Shades of SCARLET

ANNE FINE

David Fickling Books

31 Beaumont Street
Oxford OX1 2NP, UK

London Borough of Hackney	
91300001140792	
Askews & Holts	
JF YA	£12.99
	6444878

Text © Anne Fine, 2021

978-1-78845-135-2

1 3 5 7 9 10 8 6 4 2

Papers used by David Fickling Books are from well-managed forests and other responsible sources.

MIX
Paper from
responsible sources
FSC
www.fsc.org   FSC® C018072

DAVID FICKLING BOOKS Reg. No. 8340307

A CIP catalogue record for this book is available from the British Library.

Typeset in 11/18 pt Sabon by Falcon Oast Graphic Art Ltd, www.falcon.uk.com
Printed and bound in Great Britain by Clays, Ltd, Elcograf S.p.A.

How do you open the most beautiful notebook you've ever seen, and start to write in it, when you don't even know what you think? I wasn't even sure what I *felt*. I must have sat there on the window seat until my hand was sticky, holding my fine-tipped pen over the first thick, creamy page. So many excellent first sentences ran through my brain. 'My mother's the most selfish person on the *planet*.' 'My mum's an *idiot*.' 'My mother has just spoiled my life, my dad's, and – I really, really hope – her own.'

But none of them was absolutely right.

Bleh, bleh, bleh. Yadda, yadda, yadda.

It's hard to know exactly where to start. But I'm beginning with the day Mum gave me that beautiful book with the creamy blank pages. She said it was a gift, but I know better. We'd had an awful run-in on the night before.

She'd snapped at me, 'Scarlet, I'm absolutely sick of seeing your face stuck to that tiny screen!'

'Don't look, then,' I'd muttered, loud enough for her to catch what I said, but not so loud I wouldn't be able to argue that I hadn't meant her to hear.

She fought back. 'You waste hours of your life on that thing.'

'It's *my* life, though, isn't it? So shouldn't I be the one to judge what's a waste of my time?'

I kept my head down, but I was watching through the curtain of hair that fell over my face. I knew that she was in two minds about starting on the business of getting me to help to put away the shopping – whether to tell me to get off my backside and lend a hand – or skip that argument and just get on with the job herself.

In the end, she said nothing. A while ago I would have

leaped to my feet to help even before being asked. But back then, she was still going through those arguments with Dad, and I felt sorry for her. I'd listen to her telling me that her whole world was crashing down. She couldn't live with Dad another week. He was intolerable with all his silent moods. She couldn't stand another day of it. It was a living death. Bleh, bleh, bleh. Yadda, yadda, yadda.

And then one day she said that we were moving out.

'What are we *doing* here? It's *horrible.*'

It was quite obvious she just assumed that I'd be going with her. That really threw me. She had been threatening to leave for so long, I'd come to think that it would never happen. I was too startled to put up a fight. 'I'll still get time with *Dad*?'

'Of course you'll still get time with Dad. As much time as you want.'

I'd wondered what she'd say if I'd said, '*All* of it.' But she was tense, and on the edge of ratty, so I said nothing and just took a heap of my stuff along with her to that grotty little flat beside the railway station.

It didn't take even a couple of hours to regret it. 'What are we *doing* here? It's *horrible*. There's slime up all the bathroom walls. The floors are sticky. And it'll take ages for me to get to school from here.'

'It's only for two weeks, Scarlet. After that, we'll be somewhere much better.'

Suspiciously, I asked, 'How come?'

'Because a friend of mine has offered me a long loan of a very nice house.'

('A friend of mine', you notice. Not, 'a girlfriend of mine'. And, 'a very nice house'. Not, 'her very nice house'. Did Mum think I was *stupid*?)

'Why aren't we there already, then?'

'We would be, except that this morning it turned out that there was a bit of a hold-up.'

'Pity you didn't hold up a bit yourself,' I muttered, but she pretended that she hadn't heard, and went on to say that where we were going was even nicer than the house we'd been living in with Dad. 'You'll love it, Scarlet. You'll have the most wonderful bedroom up a tiny winding stair. It runs the whole length of the house. There are windows at each end – round ones, a bit like portholes on a ship, but larger. One overlooks the street, and from the other you can see everyone's back gardens. The ceiling's low and arched so it'll seem a bit like living in the cabin of your own private boat.'

'Why didn't you take me with you to see it?'

She looked a bit uneasy as she explained, 'Oh, I nipped

out in my lunch hour. There wasn't time to get you out of school and back again before your afternoon session.'

It was the first I'd ever heard of Mum having a lunch hour. She runs a hospital, and always before she'd claimed that she's rushed off her feet from the moment she walks through the hospital doors until she finally manages to get away from every last person who wants 'just one quick word before you go home, Fran'. She says she rarely finds time even to buy a sandwich in the middle of the day, let alone eat it.

So I'll admit that, with one thing and another, my antennae were definitely swirling about in the air. Next day, Dad came to fetch me for some time with him, and though I could tell that Mum was really irritated with me for doing it, I dragged him to the bathroom to show him exactly how disgusting it was. Dad shook his head, but all he said to Mum was, 'I'll tell you this, Fran. Whoever owns this place is not in line to win this year's Good Tile Grouting Awards.'

It sounded bland enough, though I did wonder if the dig packed more of a punch against somebody I didn't know about than Dad was letting on. But I was smart enough to keep my mouth shut and my eyes wide open. I knew it wouldn't be too long before I found out what was going on.

Newsflash!

It was only a day or so after we moved out of that fleapit flat into the new house that I got the story. Coming back to class after his music lesson, Pedro leaned close to whisper, 'Hey, Scarlet! Newsflash! Jake Naylor says that his dad's brother is going out with your mum.'

I must have looked an idiot, staring at Pedro with my mouth wide open. 'What's that supposed to mean?'

'Just what I said. Apparently your mum has a boyfriend, and he's—'

Et cetera. Jake Naylor's Uncle Richard.

Jake's actually in my *class*. He is a *friend*. So you can see why, when I got home that night, I stuck to my screen and wouldn't leap up ('Oh, you're a sweetie, Scarlet!') to help Mum sort out the shopping. Why should I? She had lied to everyone. All of that stuff about Dad having moods and their relationship not being 'deep enough'! Who'd be surprised, if she was off out all the time with Richard Naylor? So how could she tick me off for spending more time with my head down, staying in touch with my friends, than wanting to help her unpack the groceries?

When she held out the scarlet book, I kept my hands behind my back.

'Go on,' she said. 'Take it. I thought it was perfect for you, given your name. It's a present.'

I looked at it. Fat, thick and square, with the shiniest cover in wonderful shades of scarlet. She flipped it open to show me its blank cream pages with no schooly blue lines. I knew, at any other time, I would have *loved* it. I'd have pounced on it, saying, 'It's fabulous! Where did you *find* it?'

Instead, I scowled.

'Scarlet,' she told me warningly, 'when someone offers you a gift, it's only polite to accept it and thank them.'

I took it from her, letting the hand that held it drop to my side at once so she could see I wasn't even bothering to look at it. Coolly, I said, 'Thank you.'

'*And* say how nice it is.'

I kept my voice dead frosty. 'It's very nice.'

Mum looked around in a bit of a hunted fashion before she started up again. 'I know things haven't been easy for you these last weeks,' she said. 'All these big changes. So I thought I'd buy you this. We're starting very differently in this new house, and I thought you might like to write about your brand-new life.'

Who did she think I was? Some Jenny-No-Mates with nothing better to do but keep a daily diary?

'Thank you,' I said again, as dully as I dared. I turned

away, and holding the book by the corner as if it were greasy, or crawling with maggots or something, I carried it up here to take a better look at it without her watching to see what I thought.

No chance!

It was the classiest notebook I had ever seen – sort of flashy and cool all at the same time. It must have cost the earth. But if she thought that I was going to use it to write down what was happening in my own 'new life' and how I felt about it, then she was wrong. So wrong.

She might believe that she had thought things through, but I was still a good few steps ahead. I knew why Mum had given me the scarlet book. She wanted me to keep a diary so she could sneak up and take what she would think of as a little motherly look at it every now and again, and read what I'd written. I reckoned that it was the way she thought that she could keep her psychic tabs on me.

No chance!

Oh, I might write in it, all right. I might fill up every last page of it, and then even write more stuff all around the edges like one of those old ladies in Victorian novels. But, if I did, then I'd be using it to spill the beans about *her* life, not mine. I'd tell the truth. And not *her* version of the truth, seeing things only in the way she chose.

The truth.

And I would hide it where she'd wouldn't ever find it. No, not till I was ready to hand it over to her.

That would drive her mad.

'See if that's her.'

I told Alice what I planned to write inside Mum's sneaky present. She sounded doubtful for only a moment. 'Well, yes. I suppose, when you come down to it, she is pretty well asking for it.'

'Isn't she just?'

We almost always agree on things. I've known Alice since we were four, and met in nursery school. She told me that her mother was a spacewoman and would send me a lump of the Moon. (In fact, she teaches I.T.) And I was so jealous that I told her my dad was a magician (he works in pharmaceuticals) and on her next birthday I would persuade him to give her his big white rabbit.

I don't remember how we managed the disappointment. I just know we've been friends ever since. So she and I were coming out of school together the next afternoon when I caught a glimpse of a red car exactly like Mum's coming around the corner.

Mum never usually picks me up. I reckoned she was still trying to suck up for the upheaval she was causing everyone. I didn't feel like letting her think that I was falling in with it like some tame lamb, so I pushed Alice on ahead. 'See if that's her.'

Alice did the usual trick – wandered out through the gates, rooting deep in her bag as if to check she hadn't left something behind in our home room. Then she rushed back. 'Yes, that's your mum. She's just pulled up outside.'

'Do you think that she saw you?'

'No, she was fishing in her bag for her phone.'

'Good.'

I sent a message that I'd gone to Dad's. Then I dragged Alice back into school and out of the south door.

'So you *did* know!'

I had been thinking about my dad all day. Up till I learned the truth, I reckon I'd felt more sympathy for Mum than for him. I suppose over the months before things all blew up, I'd swallowed her lines on everything because she talked more:

'Tony, I reckon you take on extra shifts deliberately, to save yourself from having to come home and talk to me and Scarlet.'

'When do you ever start a conversation, Tony? I might as well be living with a brick *wall*.'

'When was the last time you suggested doing anything nice?'

'If I disappeared tomorrow, you'd barely notice that I wasn't here.'

Dad always muttered things like, 'Nonsense, Franny,' and, 'You know that isn't true.' But he had never fought back, and I'd assumed that was because he'd no defence to offer.

Now I was curious to know if he had just stayed quiet because he knew I might be eavesdropping. Maybe he'd known about this Richard Naylor all along. Perhaps they'd had a thousand very different conversations when they knew I was out and couldn't be listening: 'Why should I make an effort to talk to you when . . . ?' 'Who even wants to *try* to have a nice time with somebody who . . . ?'

That sort of thing, instead.

Dad works in Quality Control at Weuth Pharmaceuticals. (Alice calls it 'the Pill Factory'.) He starts at five and ends just after lunch, so I knew he'd be home. I was too jumpy to wait for the bus, so I walked back with Alice as far as her house, then borrowed her bike to get across the park.

I found Dad on the sofa, half asleep. He was surprised to see me, I could tell. 'Hi, sweetie. Change of plan, was it? Has your mother dropped you off?'

'I came on Alice's bike.'

'Problem?'

'Not really, no.' And then I thought about it. 'Actually, yes.'

He prised himself upright and I could tell it was an effort. 'What's that then, sweetpea?'

'I want to know some things.'

His face closed up a bit, although he said, 'Go on, then. Fire ahead.'

'First, did you *know*?'

'Know?'

I snapped, 'Oh, don't pretend you don't know what I'm talking about. Did you know Mum was having an affair with this bloke?'

'Richard Naylor?'

'So you did know!'

Out of a brick wall

He sighed. 'Of course I did. I'm not blind. Or stupid.'

He realized at once how what he'd said might sound, and tried to backtrack. 'I'm sorry, Scarlet. I wasn't trying to suggest you're either of those things. It's just that people your age aren't generally alert to all the little signs.'

'What little signs?'

He shrugged. 'Oh, I don't know. Small changes. More trips to the hairdresser. A different perfume. Loads more "late meetings" than usual.'

'Is that what tipped you off that something was wrong?'

He said uneasily, 'I really shouldn't be talking to you this way.'

That set me off. 'Which way?' I snapped. 'As if I have a *brain*? As if this might be something to do with *me* as well as with you two?'

'Don't get so ratty,' he said, and suddenly I realized he was sounding really tired. For the first time I noticed that he had black shadows under his eyes. 'Listen,' he said. 'It's very hard to work out how these things happen. At first, when someone's met another person who makes them happy, they tend to spread their cheerful feelings around. Your mum was really lovely for a while.'

I think he was embarrassed to hear himself say that. I watched him heaving forward to get off the sofa. 'I'll make some tea.'

'No,' I said. 'I'll make the tea. You carry on explaining.'

'Well, that's about all I have to say.'

'That things were nice for a while?' I almost parroted, adding sarcastically, 'That's where your explanation stops, is it?'

There was a silence. I put the kettle on. He found the milk. 'Go *on*!' I told him. 'Mum is so right. Getting words out of you is like trying to squeeze them out of a *brick wall.*'

'Should I have *strangled* your mother?'

That got to him. 'You stop it, Scarlet!' he said. 'I won't be criticized this way. I have done nothing except try to get us all through this without too much damage. And things *are* hard to explain because they start all topsy-turvy, seeming a whole lot better before they suddenly take a turn for the worse.'

'Worse, like before we left?'

'Yes. Worse like that. With your mum out all the time. And even when she was here, the endless nagging. "Tony, you *never* this." "You *always* that." On and on. I kept on trying – but it seemed, whatever I did, there would be something else for her to complain about.' He sighed. 'Now I look back, it's obvious she was just trying to persuade herself she had no choice but to do what she wanted to do anyhow.'

'Which was move out.'

'Which was move out.' He reached for the steaming kettle. 'Still . . .'

I pushed the mugs his way. 'What I don't get,' I told him, 'is why you didn't put up a fight.'

15

'Like how? Go out and find the man and punch his lights out? Should I have *strangled* your mother? What did you have in mind?'

'I don't know. But *something*. Instead of simply sitting on that sofa getting more and more moody.'

Another silence. Then he said, 'If I am honest, I can tell you it was a bit of a relief to have the whole ghastly business boiling over. I know that I was getting sick and tired of being the villain of the piece. At least things are quieter now.'

'For *you*.'

The look on his face was sheepish. 'I'm sure that, in the end, things will be better for you too.'

'Oh, *are* you? Are you *really*?' Before the tears could start, I hurled the mug he'd handed me onto the floor. It didn't break, but hot tea splashed all over. 'And we both know why, don't we?' As I slammed out of the door, I shouted back at him, 'Because it's *easier* for you to think that way. But it's not true!'

'Aren't parents *weird*?'

I dumped the bike in Alice's front garden. Her brother Andy opened the door. 'Hi, Scarlet.'

I guess he could tell from my face that I wasn't in the

mood for any of our usual jokey exchanges. Hastily backing his wheelchair out of my way, he nodded towards the stairs. 'She's in her room.'

Alice was no more impressed with my dad than I'd been. 'You're telling me he knew your mum was seeing someone else, and he did *nothing*?'

I threw myself on her bed. 'That's what he said.'

'And all those arguments that you kept telling us about, when she was going on at him. He never even *told* her why he was being such a grouch?'

'I never heard him say a word, even when they had no idea that I was listening.'

'Aren't parents *weird*?'

'Yours aren't,' I told her enviously.

Alice dismissed this. 'Oh, mine are weird enough. Mum's always on about the government, and Dad fusses about everything.'

'But at least your dad wouldn't say nothing at all if you went off with your mum to live in a foul, grotty flat and then a stranger's house.'

'No,' Alice said. 'And that is odd. Even if he'd been keeping quiet before, he surely should have come out with something then. He should have told you what was going on.' A thought struck Alice. 'Maybe he *didn't* know. Maybe he's just pretending now that he knew what was happening all along so you don't think that he's an idiot.'

'He knew the man's name.'

'Oh.'

We sat there gloomily for a while. Then Alice said, 'So how mad at him are you?'

'At Dad? Or Richard Naylor?'

'Your dad.'

I thought about it for a bit. Then I said, 'Pretty mad. I mean, not nearly as mad as I am at my mum, because she started all of this. She is the one who's mucked things up. But I am pretty mad at Dad.'

'Awful.'

'Yes, awful.'

'I hope you don't end up like poor old Pedro.'

'No such thing as one bad parent.'

I shuddered. Pedro sits next to Jake in some of our classes. He has a brand-new stepdad who's moved into their house and does his imitation of an angry seagull all the time. Pedro's expected to pretend he thinks it's funny. Every time. Over and over. His mum gets huffy if Pedro ever shows he's bored and leaves the room. 'You could be *nicer* to Neil,' she keeps on telling Pedro. 'More polite.' Pedro says he'd prefer to be with his dad, but no one's letting him, except on odd weekends.

'No way that I'll end up like Pedro,' I said fiercely.

I'm sure Alice believed me. We all know Pedro's a bit of a wimp. Still, she kept trying to cheer me up. 'Anyhow, I'm sure this Richard Naylor isn't a bit like Pedro's stepdad.'

'I don't care what he's like. I just don't want him in my life. I want things right back how they were.'

'Even with all that sniping between your mum and dad?'

'Even with all that. It isn't fair for them to turn things upside down like this.'

'It wasn't really your dad's fault.'

I wasn't buying that – not any more. 'I reckon it was almost as much his fault as Mum's. He didn't do a thing about it, did he? He just sat back and let it happen. He has to take some blame. He's like one of those people who watches a step-parent being spiteful to their kid and doesn't do anything about it because they don't want the hassle.' I was so angry that I clenched my fists. 'There's no such thing as one bad parent,' I declared. 'There's one *bad* parent, and the other *rubbish* one who lets it happen.'

Then I burst into all the tears that had been banked up, waiting.

'Sorr-eee.'

I had to go back to the new house in the end, of course. I dragged my feet a bit, knowing that Mum would start in on me at once: 'You saw your dad, did you? So how was he? What did he have to say?'

I wasn't in the mood to tell her anything, and even before I'd got through the door, she was complaining. 'I have to tell you, Scarlet, that you have been extremely inconsiderate! I took time off work to come and pick you up today. I didn't get the message that you'd decided to go to your dad's till I was outside the school. If I had known, I could have stayed at work and cleared my desk.'

I used the see-if-I-care, sing-song voice that drives her crazy. 'Sorr-eee.'

'No, seriously! I won't be treated like that.'

Bad move on her part. 'Like what?' I snapped. I waved my hand around to indicate the new house we were in. 'Like finding out about something important a bit too late to have any say in it? Like *that*, you mean?'

She took the point. Flushing, she turned away and made out she was looking for something in one of the kitchen cabinets. I knew the angry silence wouldn't last too long because she'd want to find out what my dad had said and how he'd been. I wasn't going to make it easy, though. The moment that she'd turned her back, I started for the hall door.

She must have sensed that I was creeping out. 'Please stay in here a moment.'

'I have a lot of homework.'

'I'm sure it can wait.'

With a great sigh, I plumped myself down at the table. 'All right, then. What do you want?'

'Please watch your tone of voice, Scarlet.'

'Sorr-eee.'

Irritated, she pulled a chair out from the table so hard its legs scraped on the floor tiles. 'So how was your father, anyway?'

I gave her the look that said, 'I don't see why that's any longer any business of yours,' and took my time to answer.

'He was all right.'

She wasn't going to let it go. 'What was he doing?'

'Nothing much.'

Her voice turned steely with warning. 'Scarlet . . .'

I wasn't going to let her pick a row with me. She'd just have felt on top. I knew that what would irritate her most was me not telling her a single thing. So I said casually, 'Just what I said. He wasn't doing much. He was just napping on the sofa when I came in, and then we made a cup of tea.'

'So did you talk about things?'

'Not really, no.'

'And what does that mean?'

She actually had the nerve to look at me as if she was expecting an answer.

She had no right to ask

It was the *cheek* of it that got to me. Did she not realize that I wasn't going to tell her anything? Perhaps she had me down for someone of six years old who'd innocently drift from one house to the other, spilling the beans to feed each parent's curiosity without ever figuring out how they were being used. She had no right to ask what Dad and I had talked about. Our conversations were now *private*. That is the choice she made when she moved out with her stuff. It left me with two separate homes, and I intended to *keep* them separate.

I didn't tell her any outright lies, but I did do an excellent job of picking a few completely useless bits and pieces out of the conversation I'd had with Dad. Not only that, but I made Mum work really hard to winkle out every single one of them, and even so, all she got at the end was a long, boring nothing: 'We talked a bit about Alice's bike.' 'He asked me about school.' 'We talked about how often people have haircuts.' 'We made tea and I spilled mine, so that had to be cleaned up.'

She tried to hide her irritation. I watched her wondering if she should put an end to what we both knew was a total farce, and ask straight out, 'Did your dad mention me?' But in the end she chickened out and simply said, 'And that was it?'

'More or less.' I scraped my chair back. 'So can I go upstairs now, please, and start my homework?'

She gave up. I could see her giving up. She looked quite helpless, if I'm honest. Almost forlorn. Shrugging, she told me, 'Supper will be in about twenty minutes.'

I felt the tiniest bit sorry for her, so I said amiably, 'That's good. Because I haven't had a thing since lunch, and now I'm starving.'

She seemed pleased at that.

Miles away from home. Both homes.

I went upstairs and messaged Alice. But she's not allowed to have her phone at the table while her family eat supper, so I gave that up as a waste of time and did the first batch of homework. Then I tugged the fitted cushion on the rounded window ledge out far enough to reach around the back and under the flap that hides the zip. I pulled out the scarlet book I'd tucked inside, pushed the cushion back in place and parked myself on top. It felt quite cosy, sitting sideways on the porthole window ledge. The branches of the nearest tree were waving away outside enough to make me feel as if I might have been somewhere windy and wild in the country.

And miles away from home. *Both* homes.

Nothing got written, though. I thought about things for a while, and wondered about Dad. When Willow's mother took Willow and her brothers away, their father started drinking. I didn't think my dad was likely to do that, but I did think he would get lonely in that house all by himself. And it was looking pretty drab. When Mum was packing, she took so much of the nice stuff. I didn't notice at first and, to be fair, she started in a reasonable way with things that she said meant a lot to her and not that much to Dad.

'Do you mind, Tony? After all, I bought it with my first month's wages.' Or, 'Aunt Maisie gave it to me years ago. I've always loved it.'

But gradually, I noticed, she got a little pushy. 'You don't want this, do you, Tony? Can I take it with me?' And, 'I've never seen you even glance at this. I'll take it, shall I?'

He didn't argue about anything. Not one single thing. I couldn't work out if he was too dumb – or maybe even numb – to notice, or if he didn't want to give Mum the satisfaction of thinking he cared about any of the shared things from their marriage that she was stashing in her boxes, ready to take away. And she had always been the one to buy the things like pictures and ornaments, and silk flowers in pretty vases. He'd left all that to her. Now so much was missing that I reckoned Dad must glance around and think the house looked dull and miserable. I know I had. I'd looked at where she'd lifted photos from the walls and left those telltale patches on the wallpaper. She'd even pinched the bright red shower curtain.

I felt a rush of worry about him sitting there with all those cheerful things gone. So I gave up on the idea of writing in the scarlet book and shoved it back inside its hiding place. Then, though I knew that it was nearly time to go downstairs to eat, I phoned him. 'Dad? Suppose I come round at the weekend? We can paint the front room.'

He sounded startled. 'Paint it? But, Scarlet, it was only wallpapered a couple of years ago.'

'I know,' I said. 'But there are all those funny patches where Mum has taken things away. It would look better.'

He didn't sound at all keen. 'It's a big job. And once you start . . .' I waited while he made up his mind. 'No, Scarlet. It's sweet of you to offer. I do appreciate that. But it would be much simpler to look for pictures the right size from a charity shop.' I reckon he was trying to convince himself as much as me, because he added, 'And that would do some good for someone else as well.'

I practically had to stop myself from hurling my phone across the room in sheer frustration. Get pictures from a charity shop? How feeble is *that*? It seemed to me that, just as Mum was getting tougher, barging along, head down, to get exactly what she wanted, Dad was becoming more and more pathetic. First, he had made no effort to face up to Mum and try to keep her. Then he had let her take me with her without any argument. 'So long as I can see Scarlet regularly, and she's allowed to come back here whenever she wants.'

Now this – Dad happy to sit stewing in a room that reeked of loneliness and failure and what-used-to-be, but turning down an offer to take one small step into a new life. 'Sorry,' I told him. 'I can't hear you properly. You've gone all faint and hissy. I'll be in touch tomorrow.'

So that was that. I stared at the phone and asked myself if I should go back there to live. Would that put more spine in him? Would he be better off if he had me for company more of the time? I knew that I could kick up such a fuss that Mum would have to let me go back to the old house if that was what I wanted.

If . . .

'Oh, yes. I'll bet.'

The call came up the winding stair. 'Scarlet! Supper time!'

I slid off the window ledge. 'Coming!'

But Mum was already in the doorway. 'Sorry,' she said. 'I wasn't sure if you could hear.'

I gave her a look that pretty well said aloud, 'Oh, yes. I'll bet,' then watched her peering nosily round the room. (Good thing I'd put away the scarlet book. I didn't want her to think that now I was on my own, I was admiring it.) After a moment, she told me something I already knew. 'You haven't even started to unpack your boxes.'

Did she expect me to *apologize*? I raised an eyebrow.

'Never mind,' she said hastily. 'I'll help you after supper. We'll get it done in no time.'

'I might not want it doing yet,' I told her coolly. 'I'm not sure that I want to keep all this stuff here. I might decide to take a lot of it back home.'

I'd hoped that calling the house we'd left 'back home' would rattle her. But she just changed the subject. 'I made carbonara.'

I wasn't going to let her put me in the wrong. 'Yummy!' I said. 'One of my favourites.'

She tried a smile, and I smiled back. They were a little forced, but just enough for us to start the supper on an even keel, without an argument.

And I was hungry. It had been a horribly long day.

'I wonder who I get that habit from.'

Of course, the truce over supper didn't last. Over the last weeks Mum had turned into a bulldozer. She couldn't wait to push her world in line exactly the way she wanted it. She started sensibly enough, asking me all about my day at school. (What's to say? School days are school days.) She asked about Alice. 'I'm pretty sure I saw her coming out of school while I was waiting for you. I would have called to her, but she dived back inside.'

'I expect she'd forgotten something.'

'I was surprised to see her, though. I thought that you two generally leave school together.'

'Not always.'

Reckoning she'd softened me up enough, she came back to the topic that was uppermost in her mind. 'So you did think your dad was all right, then?'

Why should I help soothe her guilty conscience about what she'd done to him? I waited just a moment, and then came out with a bland, 'I suppose so.' I wanted her to think that I'd have answered that way even if I'd walked in to find my dad knotting a hangman's noose and eyeing the light fittings. She'd left him, after all. So let her fret.

She didn't push the matter. All she said was, 'You're not being very forthcoming, Scarlet.'

'I suppose I'm not.'

Knowing that we were on the verge of arguing, I started shovelling pasta into my mouth. I really didn't want to have to leave the table before I'd cleared my plate.

'Please don't stuff your face like that. It's horrid to watch.'

I didn't think it was the moment to say, 'Then look the other way,' so I slowed down.

'Well?' she said, after a pause.

I looked up, all wide eyes and innocence. 'Well, what?'

'I said you weren't being very communicative. You're hardly telling me anything.'

I shoved in one last mouthful before I came out with the challenge she deserved. 'I wonder who I get that habit from.'

Her eyes had narrowed in warning. 'Scarlet . . .'

'Who's been talking to you?'

But I was ready for her. I'd known she wouldn't be able to stand my holding out on her about my feelings. (Her giving me the scarlet book had been the proof of that.) So I was ready. I'd been practising the speech on and off all day – all through Maths, all through Late Assembly and all through my last walk home.

I kept my voice down. I didn't get excited. I spoke to her as if I'd suddenly had an interesting thought. 'But, Mum, how can you complain about *me* not talking about things? Look at *you*. You obviously didn't share much with Dad about *your* feelings, because he ended up thinking the split was all to do with him not being good enough to keep the marriage going. And you've not told me *anything* about this house.' I gave her a big warm smile. 'Like who has paid for it, and who is no doubt going to come and share it with us.'

Oh, she was staring at me now. She looked quite frightened. 'What are you talking about?'

'Who,' I corrected her. 'I reckon that it's *who* we're talking about, not what. And that is Richard Naylor.'

She went bright scarlet. 'Who's been talking to you about that?'

'People at school.'

That did for her, you could tell. She sounded stunned. 'Seriously? People at *school*?'

'Why wouldn't they?' I said. 'After all, not everyone is quite as uncommunicative as you. Jake Naylor knows about it. Richard Naylor is his uncle. Perhaps Jake's said a bit too much to suit *you*. But everyone in class knows all about it now.' I pushed my plate away. 'And so do I.'

I left her sitting at the table like a rag doll with all the stuffing fallen out.

Did I feel sorry for her? Not at all.

'Permafrost.'

There was no lock on my door, so I pushed a couple of the heaviest boxes against it, to make a point if she came up.

Then I phoned Alice.

'So how's it going?' she asked at once.

'Permafrost.'

'You? Or your mum?'

'Me. We just had supper and Mum is still down there psyching herself to barge up here with all guns blazing.'

'Why?' Then Alice tumbled. 'Scarlet! You dared to tell her what you *know*? How did she take it?'

'Like a great smack in the face. And then I came up here.'

'You're brave,' said Alice. 'I think, if I'd been you and done that, I would have sneaked away, back to my dad's, till I was sure that things were safe.'

I hadn't realized, until Alice said that, how very disappointed in my dad I'd been. Till then, he'd always been the one I'd gone to when I had any sort of trouble with Mum. She is the parent who keeps tabs on me. She is the one who knows what nights I get out late from school because of clubs, and checks if I have homework, and whether or not it's been done. So she's the one who's always on my back.

But almost always, when she was mad at me, I could depend on Dad to calm things down. 'Franny, be fair. You did say Scarlet had till the end of the weekend to clear up her room. It's only five now so she still has time.' Or, 'Steady on, Fran. I'm sure that Scarlet didn't mean to be rude. It just came out that way.'

Now he was over a mile away and I was on my own.

'Well,' I said sourly, 'I'm not sure that he would have helped all that much this time. All he's done so far is sit tight and hope the problem will go away.'

'And now you and your mum have gone, instead.'

She didn't mean it in a jokey way, so the short laugh I let out probably did sound bitter. To make it clear that she was on my side, she added flatly, 'And now you're stuck there with your mum in that new house.'

I had the oddest feeling of being really irritated with Alice. Oh, I knew she was only trying to sympathize; but no one really likes to hear their best friend saying they are 'stuck' with their mum.

Alice has spent a huge amount of time with me and my family. Mum's always liked her, and Alice always got on fine with her. When Andy got smashed up in that car crash, Alice stayed in our house for weeks while Mr and Mrs Henty spent most of their time at the hospital. And even after her brother was well enough to come back home, Alice still slept at our house often.

My mum was really good to her for all that time.

I don't think Alice realized that what she'd said was bothering me so much. She just kept on. 'And now you're having to sit there, waiting for her to come up and give you a lecture?'

'That's about it.'

'She does the dirty and you get the telling-off.' She sighed. 'These things are so *complicated*. Didn't your dad have *any-thing* helpful to say when you were round there?'

Suddenly Mum was coming up the winding stairs.

'Got to go, Alice. Visitor!'

'Don't you know *anything* about grown-up feelings?'

She got the message and hung up at once. So by the time that Mum had shoved the door so hard that the boxes slid to the side, I was just sitting quietly with my knees up in the porthole window seat, shuffling a few sheets of paper to make it look as if I was sorting out something to do with my schoolwork.

'Problem?' I asked her, in the exact same way she says the word to me when I burst in on her because of network connection troubles, or needing money for something.

She didn't answer at first, just stood by the unpacked boxes looking a little uncertain. Then she perched on the edge of the bed. 'I've an apology to make to you,' she said.

I didn't ask her what about. I simply waited, staring at the sheets of paper in my hand.

'It's about Richard. About not telling you. About you having to hear about it through rumours at school.'

'Rumours?' I beamed at her spitefully. 'So it's not true then? You're *not* having an affair with some bloke called Richard Naylor? It's all some stupid rumour I picked up at school, with no truth to it at all? Oh, I'm so *plea—*'

'Stop it!' she spat at me. 'Stop that right now. I can't be doing with this childish sarcasm. For God's sake, Scarlet! You sound about three! Don't you know *anything* about grown-up feelings?'

That one went home. Of course I know about them. I'm in a class of twenty-two, and at the last count only thirteen of us had both the parents that we started off with still living with us under the same roof. (It would be only twelve now, I realized suddenly.) So I know all about people her age and their *feelings*. I know they probably all got married thinking that they were madly in love and it would last for ever, like in a fairy tale. I know a lot of the women even changed their names, as if they weren't just handing themselves over, but giving up their personalities as well. I bet huge numbers of them were silly enough to spend all their savings having the fanciest wedding they could imagine. Some of the women probably went hysterical if there was even a suggestion of rain or wind, in case it mussed their hair. They probably burst into tears if the florist turned up with flowers the wrong colour.

Basically, I expect a lot of them went bats.

Then they had children – everyone in our year group. But while we've all been working our way up the school, things have been changing. So I know all about relationships that have 'gone stale'. Like bread! And about people like Pedro's mum, who suddenly fell head over heels in love with someone else. I know that Mia's mum went on a pilgrimage to Santiago de Compostela to 'consider her options', and came back with a girlfriend. And Willow's mum took off with no excuse at all except that she was 'bored'. (I bet she's less bored now that she has Willow and her brothers all the time because Mr Parker's ended up taking to drink.) Then there are people like Greg's dad, offered some wonderful new job in Dubai. He claimed the salary would pay off the mortgage in no time, and make all their lives a whole lot easier. Except that he didn't ever send home any money, and then he never came back. Greg and his mother have had to live with Greg's foul-tempered grandfather for two years now.

And they're not the only people I know who've had their lives turned upside down – some more than once.

'Go on, then,' I said, not even bothering to hide the sarcasm. 'Do tell me all about your grown-up feelings.'

'Oh, really!' But it was clear to her that either she had to flounce straight out again, which would have got her nowhere, or take the chance of trying to explain to me something of what was in her mind.

I had to hand it to her. She had a go. 'Scarlet, I cannot tell you how sorry I am that this has happened. You're very young. You probably won't understand. Obviously, you adore your dad, and you can't see how anyone in their right mind would want to dump a marriage that lasted nearly twenty years.'

I didn't say a word, but I did finally put down the sheets of schoolwork.

'I love your father still,' she told me. 'I always will. He's a good man. He's never in his life been nasty with me, or with you. He's been an excellent provider. You cannot fault him.'

I was so tempted to break in and say, 'I wasn't trying to fault him. That always seemed to be *your* job.' But I held my tongue.

'But,' she said, 'everyone only gets one life. Just one. And it's so difficult if you come to realize that you're not living it in the right way. Or with the right person.' She brushed aside the words she guessed were in my mind. 'Oh, I know that your father must have been the right person once. And probably for a good deal of the time we were together. But he's not right for me now. And that might not have mattered. We'd probably just have batted on the same way we always had until . . . until . . .'

She found it difficult to get his name out, so I said it for her.

'Until this Richard Naylor came along.'

Perhaps she mistook my finishing the sentence for her for a bit of sympathy. 'Exactly! It's easy to do without something important if you don't even realize that it's an option. But once it comes along . . .'

I hid the sarcasm. 'Practically handed to you on a plate . . .'

'And you know, just *know* . . .'

'Of course!' I said. 'I understand. Of course I do. It's just like when I knew, just *knew*, that I would never, ever, ever be happy again unless I had a pony.' I let my mouth drop open in mock amazement. 'Oh, sorry!' I corrected myself. 'Mistake! Because I never did get a pony, did I? You told me that my life would go on pretty well without one. And miracle of miracles, it did!'

I couldn't stand the way she looked at me then. I turned my eyes back to the sheets of paper propped against my knees.

She said to me, 'I'll leave you to get on with your work.' It was impossible to work out from her tone of voice what she was thinking. She took one more look at the unpacked boxes, and then went out, shutting the door behind her quietly.

I will admit it. I felt like a worm.

Half a laugh. Half a sob.

By bedtime, I was starving. After all, I'd barely finished my first plate of carbonara before I'd picked that row with her. I'd had no second helping, and no pudding after. I knew I'd never sleep unless I went down to the kitchen to snaffle something. I waited till I was pretty sure she'd gone into her bedroom. All of the lights were off. It took an age to creep downstairs because I didn't yet know which parts of the floors were likely to creak when I put my weight on them. I wasn't even sure where the walls ended and the doors began.

I made it, though. I slid the biscuit tin closer, and prised off the lid. I put at least half a dozen into my dressing-gown pocket, along with a banana and two fat apples from the fruit bowl. I even opened the fridge and took out the cheese to cut myself a lump. The dishwasher was already swishing away, so I wiped the knife I'd used on a tea towel to get rid of the greasy smears, and slid it back in the drawer.

Then I crept back up the stairs.

I had got halfway up my own little winding staircase when I heard that funny little noise.

Half a laugh. Half a sob. What was she doing?

Holding a hand against the wall in the dark, I listened hard. Oh! She was on the phone. Clearly this Richard Naylor had managed to make her laugh through her tears. 'Oh, I *know*,' I heard her saying. 'I know. You're absolutely right.'

There was a bit of a pause while he presumably pedalled on a bit about why she shouldn't let herself be bothered by whatever it was that her spiteful daughter had said. 'You're right,' I heard her telling him again. 'I shouldn't push things. I should back off a bit. Give her some time.'

I stood there thinking, 'You can give me a hundred years and I will still hate what you've done, and reckon it was mean and selfish of you to do it.' And I was furious with this man who thought he had the right to say one single word to her about how she should deal with me. We'd never even met! He didn't know the first thing about me – what I was like, or how I felt, or *anything*. How dare he spoon out all this soothing advice about me to my own mother?

I was about to rush back down to burst into her room. I would have snatched the phone from her and said, 'Don't talk about me to a perfect stranger!'

I'd actually already turned when I heard what she said next. 'I know, I know! You're right. Still, it was *horrible*. It was as if she wasn't our child any more.'

Our child? Could she be talking to my *dad*?

A weird old business

I suppose I knew that being married is a weird old business. I know that parents have a sort of private language. And I don't mean like Asha's parents, who talk in Hindi if they don't want Asha to understand. (The only Hindi Asha knows is her own name, which means 'hope', and *'Thotha chana baje ghana'*, which means *'A hollow lentil makes the most noise*'.) The private language I mean is when parents talk above your head about someone who 'sounds like that landlady who caught you pushing her cat off the wall', or maybe about some actress: 'You know! The one with frizzy hair who looks like that girl your brother wanted to marry.' And since the people they are talking about probably vanished from their lives even before you were born, you haven't the faintest clue what they're describing.

They have a married way of getting at one another too. My mum would say something like, 'You really do enjoy that quiz programme, don't you?' But what she meant was, 'For God's sake, Tony! You spend far too much time watching that stupid rubbish.' And Dad might root in the shopping bag that she'd brought home and lift out a tub of bean curd. He'd hold it up to read the label. 'Tofu, eh?' was all he'd actually say. But Mum and I both knew that what he meant was, 'I sincerely hope you're not expecting me to eat this stuff, because I know right now that I won't like it.'

Those sorts of comments were all right. At least they never really soured the atmosphere. But if the two of them were in a real mood with one another, they could both turn it up a notch. 'All right, then,' he would say about some decorating job they couldn't agree on how to tackle. 'If that's the way you want to do it, fine. We'll do it your way.'

What he meant was, 'Fran, you are making a huge mistake here. *Huge*. It's going to look a *mess*.'

But she could give as good as she got about decisions like that. If she was irritated with him, she'd let her voice go distant and say, 'Oh, you decide. I don't care. Either way.' But he would have to have been dumb as a box of frogs to believe her, because what she really meant was, 'I'm so fed up with this discussion that you are going to have to *guess* what I want. And I can warn you, you had better guess right.'

They knew one another's patterns and habits backwards. 'Your father hates the Sunday morning shift.' 'Your mother will be spitting tintacks when she gets back from this meeting.' They could read one another's moods as easily as they breathed. I'd known that that would carry on at least for a while after they'd split. How could it just stop dead? And I suppose I'd guessed that they'd keep on doing one or two other things they've always done together, like discussing anything important to do with me.

But it had never occurred to me that, after she'd moved out, they might still be so thoroughly entwined that Dad would be the one she'd turn to for comfort when I had upset her.

Or that he'd still be able to come up trumps and make her laugh.

'Perhaps they will.'

'Perhaps they'll get back together,' said Alice next morning when I told her all about what I had overheard.

'Perhaps they will,' I said. I made myself sound doubtful, but deep inside I really thought – and hoped – it might be possible. If they'd both made a mistake – if Mum had been too quick in making up her mind to leave, and Dad now realized that he'd been an idiot to let her go, then maybe everything would be all right. This Richard Naylor would have to find somebody else to move into the house he'd bought. Or he could sell it. Mum would move back with all the pictures and the red shower curtain. And we could go on as we had before.

That's what I was thinking anyhow. So I was in a fairly cheerful mood when we walked through the school gates. Alice peeled off towards the Music Pod to have her flute lesson, and almost at once The Menu pounced. (His proper name is Philip. We call him The Menu because he eats so sloppily that people standing in the queue for second sitting can guess the hot meal of the day from looking at his shirt as he walks out.)

43

He was his usual upbeat self. 'Hi, Scarlet. Just one more day till Friday.'

Together we walked behind the two long lines of parked staff vehicles. There must have been a downpour overnight, along with quite a wind, because most of the cars looked pretty grubby. I hung about while he wrote I HATE PEAS in the grime on the back window of Mrs Tanner's car. (She teaches Nutrition.) Then we went in to registration.

For once, Alice came out of her music lesson dead on time. While she was jamming her flute case back in her over-stuffed locker, she said, 'You reckon that your dad cheered up your mum last night. But how were things this morning?'

'Not too bad,' I admitted. 'She had some paperwork to get through before she took off, and I pretended I had homework to finish. Nothing got said over breakfast.'

'That's good.'

'And I go straight to Dad's tonight.'

'Won't that be easier?'

I shrugged. It didn't seem to me that anything was easier. 'I suppose so. At least with Dad it's pretty well impossible to pick a fight. So it'll be a quiet night.'

'Quiet?' We both knew perfectly well that I meant boring. I watched Alice wrestling with herself about what to say next. She's heard enough from friends in separated families to know that backing out of time that you're supposed to spend with Parent No 1 is all too easily taken as siding with

44

Parent No 2. But she still ended up suggesting it: 'Do you want to blow off your dad and come to our house instead?'

It was so *tempting*. By any standards, Alice's family can't be called quiet or boring. Her parents spend the whole of every mealtime fiercely arguing with one another about things that no one else is bothered about at all: who should or shouldn't be co-opted onto the board of school governors; how much of the stuff that we recycle actually gets used; whether the Quakers really believe in God the way that people in other religions do. The two of them sit at opposite ends of their long kitchen table, so it's like watching tennis. Your head swivels this way and that till you feel dizzy. Once, when Andy was still in that horrid thick neck brace of his, he actually asked if one of them would swap seats with Alice so he could carry on watching them slug it out about whether the local park gates should or shouldn't be chained shut at night without causing himself so much pain.

But I felt sorry for my dad. I don't believe he actually sits there ticking off the hours till I show up. But I still knew I would feel guilty if I gave my evening with him a miss.

'I'd better not. Dad might have sorted something.'

'Going out to eat, maybe? Or seeing a film?'

Her spooning out these cheerful possibilities reminded me how much my dad had changed since Alice spent those weeks with us after Andy's accident. Then, he was always thinking of fun things to do because both of my parents were doing their very best to keep Alice from feeling homesick. But I didn't want to say, 'No, Dad's quite different now. I expect we'll be moping on the sofa, endlessly talking about whether to send out for pizza or Chinese.'

I was relieved when Dr Deiss swept in the room and told us all to stop talking. I like French. I have liked it ever since I was taught how to ask for chocolate ice cream when I was four years old. I think that by the time we actually started to learn French in school, I knew the words for all my favourite foods. And since that's what our classes started with – words for nice food – I had a great head start. In fact, I was such a show off I even started calling Philip 'Le Menoo' in the correct French way.

It was a good lesson, and went on till break. And then came double Maths, but since our Miss Harper was away on a course, we got to do easy worksheets. We had first sitting lunch. Pedro amused us with an imitation of his stupid stepfather doing his stupid imitation of an angry seagull. And the art lesson in the afternoon was as much of a walk in the park as usual.

So I was fine till I reached my old home.

'Oh, not *again*.'

Just glancing through the window, I could see Dad stretched full-length on the sofa with his eyes closed. Maybe it wasn't very nice of me. Or fair. He does set his alarm clock for ten past four to be at work by five. But I still slid my key into the lock so quietly he didn't hear me come in.

I hung up my jacket and pushed open the living-room door. 'Oh, not *again*,' I muttered, loud enough that if he were even halfway awake he would be bound to hear it.

Even before he opened one eye, the smile spread over his face. It was the look that he always had when I was in my first school, and came down grumpy in the mornings. 'Oho!' he'd say to no one in particular. 'What shade of Scarlet are we having today?'

But this time he did ask what set me off. 'Oh, not again *what*?'

'Nothing.'

'No, go on. Tell your old dad.'

I half disguised a sigh, then told him, 'It wasn't anything. Really, I suppose, just coming over here and finding you asleep.'

He could have fought back, saying, 'I *always* take a nap when I get home. And so would you, if your day started half as early as mine.' (Mum would have made the point sharply enough if she had overheard me.) But all Dad did was swing both legs round to the floor and say, 'I'm sorry, Scarlet. Bad day for you, was it?'

That bugged me even more – that he was being even nicer just because I'd been catty. But I couldn't stop. 'It's been fine . . .' I said, making sure both of us could hear the words I'd left unsaid float around the room: '. . . up until *now*.'

Dad flattened his palms on his knees to lever himself off the sofa. 'I'll make some tea. On my way home, I picked up a couple of those strawberry tarts you like so much.'

That made me feel even more mean. To get those strawberry tarts, he must have had to drive to Penny's Place – way off his usual route. I pulled myself together and, remembering what Alice had suggested, I said a lot more cheerfully, 'I thought that maybe tonight we could do something different.'

'Different?'

'Well, out of the house.'

'Out of the house?'

The blank way he repeated it, you'd have thought I'd said 'up on the Moon'. I felt my irritation level shoot up again. What was so mind-blowing about the idea of going out? Would it be so extraordinary to see a film? Or go to Spice

Island? I didn't have to eat the strawberry tarts right then. I could take them to school with me next morning – one for me, one for Alice.

Even the sight of him shuffling through to the kitchen annoyed me so much I pretended I'd had a message. 'Sorry, Dad. Someone in class wants to know how to do the homework, and all my notes are upstairs.'

I only realized as I shut my bedroom door that I had hurried away from him just the way Mum used to do. She used to make a break for it each time he irritated her with his lukewarm response to all suggestions that the two of them might do something out of their usual routine. I'd even sympathized with her. As soon as I'd found out about Richard Naylor, of course, I felt very differently and had a deal more sympathy for Dad, what with his horribly early mornings, a full day at work, and still being expected to make an effort to provide an interesting evening.

But that night, when I ran upstairs, I realized I was back to thinking he was just being pathetic.

Strawberry tarts

I messaged Alice and stayed upstairs, trying to make my bedroom look less bare by shunting around some of the things I'd left behind. Shells I picked up a thousand years ago on holiday beaches. A few old rings and necklaces and bracelets I never wear. Last year's school notebooks. My curly-toed Arabian slippers. Even my dried up loofah with the weird end that looks like a dismal face. (It is so creepy that it used to haunt me, but I can't throw it away.)

Less than five minutes later, Alice was back in touch. 'Scarlet! How's it going?'

I didn't try to pretend. 'Not too well. I've hardly been back for half an hour and I just want to kick him.'

'Why? What's he done?'

'Nothing. That's the whole *point*.' I wanted to moan about him, so I left out mention of the strawberry tarts. 'No wonder Mum kept getting so annoyed with him. The only thing he wants to do is lie on the sofa and mope.'

'Perhaps he's depressed.'

'He's certainly depressing me.'

As usual, Alice came up trumps. 'You still have time to come over. We won't be eating until half past six, and—' She broke off. 'Hang on!'

I heard Andy's muffled voice through all the clattering around her, and Alice corrected herself. 'No, supper's at six tonight because Ben has footie.'

I checked the time. I could just do it. Just.

'Can I say I'd forgotten that your family was expecting me?'

'Sure. If it helps.'

I thought it would.

Then I went down. My dad was in the kitchen.

'Dad . . . ?'

'Scarlet?'

'Alice just rang to remind me . . .'

I broke off. There he was, standing beside the tray he'd loaded with the tea things and the strawberry tarts. He'd obviously been waiting for me to come downstairs again.

I couldn't do it. I couldn't be so mean.

He prompted. 'What? Alice rang to remind you . . . ?'

I shook my head. 'Nothing.'

'Must have been something, Scarlet. Just spit it out.'

I had to think of something. Letting on to someone that you've been planning to bunk out of spending time with them is quite as hurtful, I should think, as doing it. Probably worse, in fact, since you would still be there and they would have to keep up a brave face. So I said the first thing that came to mind. 'Alice rang to remind me that I keep having to borrow her bike because my brake blocks are gone.'

'Not any more,' he told me cheerfully. 'I got some new ones on the way to buy the tarts.'

'So we can get it done?'

'It's fixed already,' he said. 'I did it first thing after I got home.'

'Really?' I put my arms round him and hugged him tight,

reminded that he's my easy-going, never-starts-an-argument dad, and he does everything he can for me. Fine, so he wasn't what my mother wanted any more. He hadn't enough fire. He was an unexciting man in a dead boring routine that suited him.

But it had suited her as well until that Richard Naylor came along.

I didn't say another word about going out – either to Alice's, or a film, or to Spice Island. I settled on the sofa, and we watched telly while I scoffed both tarts. Then I did homework. After that we spent an amiable half hour cheating one another at cards while we discussed whether to order pizza, curry or Chinese.

By the time that the curries were delivered, we'd watched two episodes of *Not Going Out* and started on *Peep Show*.

Dad had just offered to scrub the rogan josh stains off the sofa cover while I had a bath when the phone rang. I could tell it was someone from the Pill Factory. Dad listened for a moment, then raised a finger at me, 'Scarlet, hold off that bath until I've sorted this.'

I heard him say, 'It really isn't very convenient. My daughter's with me and there's no one else to stay and mind her.'

Mind her? You'd think that I was only *three*.

'I'm fine,' I told him, loudly enough that whoever it was at the other end would hear me. That clearly made the mystery voice sound even more determined. In the end, Dad had to crack. 'Well, I suppose I could. I had a nap. But if it's a full overnight shift, I'd have to ask my daughter if she minds going back to her mother's.'

He sounded doubtful. But it was getting late in any case, and Mum's place was nearer school. Not such an early start, and more of my clothes were there. What was to lose?

'I don't mind,' I assured him. 'I was just off upstairs. And you'd be gone by breakfast anyhow.'

'That's true.' He spoke into the phone. 'All right. I'll drop my daughter off, and be with you in half an hour.'

When I came down with my school stuff, he was already in the hall, dangling his keys. 'I'm really sorry, Scarlet. That was the duty officer. She said Sajid's mum's had another stroke, so he can't do his shift.'

'It doesn't matter,' I told him. 'We had a really nice evening.'

That cheered him up. 'Yes, we did, didn't we?' As I walked out, he started switching off the lights. 'And since I'm dropping you at the other house, shall we take your bike over?'

'Good plan,' I said.

Then I looked at his tired face. He was so generous, not just doing the favour for Sajid, but always trying to make things easier for me. Some of the people in my class have to sneak things from one place to another to stop their parents getting huffy, or making scenes: 'I bought you that, so it should stay in *this* house.' That sort of thing.

So, 'No,' I said. 'On second thoughts, I think that I would rather keep the bike here with you. At home.'

He didn't see me watching

I thought that Mum looked startled when I walked through the door. I told her about Sajid's mum, and Dad taking over his shift. I thought, when I made for the stairs, she'd think of some excuse to call me back and ask about my evening. But she just said, 'You're off to bed now, are you?'

'Bath first.'

'Try not to stay up too long. It's quite late. School in the morning.'

I didn't think a thing about it, running my bath. I picked up some weird cartoon book that Mum had left on the cork stool, and flicked through that. I ran more hot in twice.

Then I got out and went to bed.

I still don't know what woke me. Or why, when I got out of bed, I padded to the window that overlooked the street.

I hadn't turned on any lights. So when he looked back at the house as he was leaving, he didn't see me watching.

'*And* staying in.'

Alice was quite excited by the news. 'You've *seen* him? What did he look like?'

I made a face. 'Can't really say. That street light's feeble. It makes everyone look a bit creepy.'

'Creepy? Ooh!' Alice shuddered with delight. 'You think he might be *creepy*?'

'I didn't say that. I just said he looked a little creepy in that weird orange light.'

I watched, getting more and more irritated as Alice hunched her shoulders and curled her fingers to try to look like a vampire. She put on a ghoulish voice. 'The creepy creep looked creepy, creeping away at night . . .'

I didn't like the way that she was making a joke of it. 'He can't be all that creepy,' I told her sharply, 'if my mum's going out with him.'

'*And* staying in.'

I had been trying not to think of that. I reckoned I had turned my bedside light off just after half past ten. It was past two in the morning when I woke up and saw him leave. I don't know what time he'd arrived, or what they did.

Maybe he just came in and sat with her in the kitchen over a late-night cup of tea. Maybe they moved through onto the brand-new sofa and kissed and cuddled.

And maybe they went to bed.

She'd left my father, after all. She hadn't gone to all that trouble just to drink tea with someone else. There was no need for that. All the time we'd been living at our old house, she had spent hours with Henry Maddox from next door. I'd burst in from my Saturday morning swimming class to find the two of them sitting over their endless cups of coffee at the kitchen table and rabbiting on about how hard it was to grow celeriac, or what a nuisance it was that the best weedkiller in the world had just been banned.

Often I'd leave them droning on about peach rot or potato blight and go upstairs to find Dad napping on my bed.

He'd open one eye. 'Sweetie, you're back. So how was swimming?'

It was such a stupid question, I'd ignore it. I'd dump my damp towel on the floor and wait for him to tell me whichever joke Sajid had passed on at the change of shift. (There's always at least one.) Then, while I was kicking off my shoes, Dad used to lever himself off my bed and ask, 'Is it safe to go downstairs yet?'

'No, Henry's still here. How did you manage to sneak up here without him seeing you?'

'He was so busy going on about that new garden centre on the bypass that he didn't hear me come in.'

Finally Henry would push off home, and Dad would come downstairs to get told off. 'Tony, I'm *sure* that Henry knew that you'd come back to the house. You ought at least to poke your head around the door and say hello to him before sneaking up for your nap.'

No. Definitely nothing going on there.

This Richard Naylor was another matter. But no one wants to imagine their mum or dad being lovey-dovey even with one another, let alone with some stranger. I wasn't going to think about it. Maybe it was a bit babyish, like clapping your hands over your ears and chanting, 'Blah, blah, blah!' when you don't want to hear what someone's saying. But I put a stop to Alice's suggestive smirk by saying, 'Well, there'll be nothing going on tonight because I will be there to watch him leave.'

'How come?'

'Because Mum says he's coming by to meet me.'

I saw the way she rolled her eyes, and it annoyed me even more. I've told you half our class come from split homes. So why should my best friend suddenly start to act as if this Richard Naylor must be some sort of gruesome monster that no one in her right mind would want her mother to invite to the house?

Isn't that my job?

Yes. I think it is.

'Whatever.'

The trouble was, I hadn't needed to be introduced to him so soon. That was my fault because, in the morning, I'd been a bit too keen to show Mum that she couldn't pull the wool over my eyes. While she was flapping round the house trying to find her phone, her office keys, her files, her notes for meetings, I'd leaned against the banisters and said, as casually as if I were asking what we would have for supper, 'So what time did your Richard Naylor leave last night?'

That threw her totally. She went beet-red. 'Richard?'

'Yes. He was here.' I paused a beat. 'Wasn't he?'

I watched her hesitate, wondering if I was bluffing. Her mouth half opened once or twice, as if she was about to speak and then thought better of it. Finally she said, 'I didn't realize you had heard him coming in.'

I gave her the look that she gives me whenever I reply with such a roundabout non-answer to something she's asked me. I watched her brace herself to tell the next whopper. 'Yes, Richard did pop round briefly. I think he came in hopes of meeting you.'

'*That* late at night?'

She bit her lip, but persisted. 'It was a bit daft, I admit, expecting you still to be up. Especially on a school night. I suppose he just didn't think. But Richard's never had kids of his own.'

'Or hasn't ever met anyone who has?'

She didn't respond to that. How could she? You only have to live on the planet for five short minutes to know that every parent in the world spends pretty well all the evening trying to edge their children into bed, or, at the very least, get them upstairs. Instead, she moved towards me for a farewell hug. I took a step back. 'Hadn't you better go?' I warned. 'You were just saying that you might be late.'

There was a long, uncomfortable pause before she said, 'All right then, Scarlet. I take your point. What I just said was nonsense. Richard did come round last night, and very late, and it was not to see you.'

I gave a knowing smirk. But she had turned away to lift her jacket off its peg. She kept on, 'But this is horribly awkward – you knowing he exists, and Richard knowing about you, and the two of you still not having so much as laid eyes on one another.' She gathered up her keys and files and made for the door. 'You'll have to meet him some time. I think I'll ask him to come round tonight.'

I felt a rush of horror. But I was quite determined to play it cool. I wasn't going to beg her, 'Oh, please don't! I'd absolutely *hate* to meet your creepy boyfriend! Do me a favour and keep him out of this house until I'm safely up in my room. Or, better still, over at Dad's!'

So all I did was shrug as if I couldn't care one way or the other and make a face that said, *Your problem, Mum. Nothing to do with me.*

'Whatever.'

She absolutely *hates* me saying that. But she was already late. So after the usual hurried nag about my being sure to leave in good time for school, and locking the house up properly behind me, my mum was gone.

Communication Skills

It was pure accident that Jake Naylor and I were paired together that day. I had been sitting beside Alice. We were about to do some dumb 'Communication Skills' exercise of Mrs Bennet's. She had been going on about how easily people misunderstand what others say, and suddenly decided that what she planned would work far better if none of us was working with our very best friend.

So, once she'd shifted a few people around, I ended up with Jake. We followed her command to twist our desks till we were facing one another. 'So you can't see the drawing that your partner will describe.'

Mrs Bennet came round the room, handing a piece of stiff card to one of each pair. ('Don't let your opposite number catch even a glimpse of it!') She gave a blank sheet of paper to the other person. ('Be warned. This is the only one you're going to get.')

Then she explained. 'The person holding the design has to describe it using only words. No peeking or showing or tracing in the air. Their partner has to draw it. And don't try to guess what it is that your partner is describing because these aren't pictures of anything in particular. They're more like diagrams because this is an exercise in the skills of accurate description and careful listening. It has nothing to do with copying.'

She checked we all had everything we needed. Then, 'Off you go,' she said.

And off we went.

Jake had the picture. He seemed to stare at it for a long time. I got a bit restless. How complicated could it be?

'All right,' he said at last. 'Here's a sort of overall description. Imagine a sort of pushchair on a sort of table top. The handles of the pushchair stick out so they almost look like the stalks of things that are a bit like cherries. And then there are some boat-sail type things to the side of that. And a circle on top of the whole lot.'

I didn't think I would start snapping at him quite so soon. '*Where* is the table top?'

Jake looked a bit baffled. 'What do you mean, *where*?'

'Where on the *paper*? A little way up? Halfway up?'

'Oh, right. I get you. More sort of halfway up the paper.'

'Big table? Small table? Wide table? Stumpy-legged table?'

He stared at the drawing in front of him again, as if for the very first time. 'Well, it's not really any of those, Scarlet.'

I was getting frustrated with him. 'Fine, Jake! Let's begin with the basics, shall we? Round table? Square table? Rectangular table?'

'Oh, rectangular!' he said, as if I should have known that from the start.

I drew a rectangular table top halfway up the paper. 'Legs?'

'What about them?'

I gritted my teeth. 'Would you care to describe them a little?'

'Well, they're just table legs.'

'Thin?' I said icily. 'Thick? Short? Long? Rounded?'

He got the point at last. 'OK, OK! They're sort of squat and short.'

I drew four short, squat legs. 'Shall we move on to what you call "a sort of pushchair" on this "sort of table top". What kind of pushchair? Do you mean the posh kind that looks like a comfy bed on wheels? Or one of those thin, spindly, folding things?'

Again he spent an age inspecting the drawing before admitting apologetically, 'Well, neither of those really.'

'Oh, get a grip!' I snapped. 'And what was all that stupid stuff about things that "almost look like the stalks of things that are a bit like cherries"? What were you on about there?'

'It's really hard to describe.'

That's when I lost my temper and snarled, 'That's the whole *point*! This is Communication Studies! You're supposed to make an effort to describe it clearly so I can *draw* the stupid thing. We haven't even started on all that stuff about "boat-sail type things" on the side? *Which* side? *Right* side? *Left* side? *Both* sides? You're *rubbish* at communicating, Jake. Pure *rubbish*!'

'Jesus!' he said. 'I hope for my uncle's sake that your mother has less of a temper!'

I stood up, reached across the desks and slapped him. Hard.

'So? Want to call it quits?'

Mrs Bennet didn't see exactly what happened. And no one split on me. But I was still sent to the office for starting what she took to be a bit of a scuffle. Miss Sinton asked me to explain, but all I told her was that Jake got on my nerves with his pathetic describing. She called him in to give his side of things. But when he realized I hadn't said a word about him mentioning his uncle and my mum, he guessed at once I wanted to keep that private.

All he said to Miss Sinton was, 'I'm not surprised that Scarlet lost her temper. It was a tricky design, and I did a rubbish job of trying to describe it. I think I might have boiled over too, if I'd been her.'

Miss Sinton told me to apologize to Jake, then ordered us back into class. Halfway along the corridor, he muttered, 'Scarlet, I'm sorry I said what I did.'

'And I'm sorry I lost it.'

We both knew I'd apologized to him already. But orders to say sorry that come from On High don't really count. This time he knew I meant it. He turned to grin at me. 'So? Want to call it quits?'

'Quits,' I agreed.

He tried to cheer me up. 'At least you'll have a good time with my uncle. He can be a real laugh.' We'd reached the classroom door. Jake turned to face me. 'We go in smiling, then?'

'Done deal.'

We went in smiling as agreed, only to find the class already grinning back like a pack of chimpanzees. It seems that Mrs Bennet had called time on the exercise. Drawings had been exchanged, and everyone had fallen about laughing at the extraordinary gap between what people thought they had described, and what their partners had drawn. Then Mrs Bennet had started to sum up the lesson. Right at the moment Jake and I walked through the door, she happened to be saying, 'See how a simple lack of good communication can ratchet up the tension? And sometimes a lack of common understanding can even lead to *violence*.'

You can imagine how much sniggering began when Jake and I walked in.

What kind of dim bulb?

Jake's uncle didn't come round that evening – not to meet me or see Mum. Mum said that he was 'very keen, but rather busy'. I didn't buy that. I reckoned he was either scared to death at the idea of facing someone he fancied's daughter, or Mum had taken fright at being rumbled, and was just keeping up a front when she told me that she'd invited him.

I didn't honestly care which. I was just glad that we were on our own. We got on pretty well, considering. I told her about Mrs Bennet's lesson (though not about my slapping Jake). She told me something that I never knew about my gran. 'She was obsessed with toilet rolls. Completely obsessed. She had a thing about how you should always hang the roll so that the free edge dangles away from the wall. Your father used to torment her terribly. He always turned it round.'

'Just to annoy her?'

'That's right. She'd put the roll back round the other way, and he'd sneak in and change it.' Mum laughed. 'He kept that up for years.'

'What, even after he left home and married you?'

'Until she died. I always thought, if we were visiting, he seemed to make a lot of trips upstairs. I just assumed his old home made him nervous. But it turned out that, all that time, he was just fighting the old battle with his mother.'

'It doesn't sound like Dad at all.'

'Oh, I don't know,' she said. 'Haven't you ever noticed that there's a sort of petty-mindedness that always sets your father off?'

I tried to read her face. I know that I was wanting to ask how she could always think such good-natured things about my dad, and still walk out on him. But while I was trying to work out how best to put it without sounding rude, she pushed my school bag further away across the table and said, 'We must get on! The freezer's full. What do you feel like eating?'

I chose lasagne and helped her make the salad. While the dish heated through, she found a cotton reel of the best matching colour and fixed the badge peeling off my school blazer. After, we watched a film. Mum stayed off her phone all evening, so I'd no reason to think she'd made any arrangement with Richard Naylor for him to come round after I'd finally disappeared upstairs. (That really would have annoyed me, as if she'd just been sitting there, being nice, but waiting for me to vanish.)

And then, next morning, she just ruined things between us once again. As she was gathering up her stuff to leave for work, she said, 'Friday! Of course! So you'll be going to your dad's tonight?'

She made it sound as if the thought had only just occurred to her. What kind of dim bulb did she think I was? Nobody lets a boyfriend lend them what I was guessing was an almost rent-free house, and doesn't know perfectly well when they'll next see one another! It's a no-brainer that that will be the very next time she can be pretty sure she'll be alone.

I wondered about coming back at her with something catty, like, 'I thought that you and Richard Naylor would be counting the hours,' or, 'Oh yes, don't worry. You and your precious Richard will be safe.'

But even in my head those two responses sounded pretty childish. So in the end I thought I'd put the wind up her by answering cheerfully, 'Yes, just so long as Dad's shift isn't changed again at the last minute.'

If I'd unnerved her with this threat that I might turn up again at any time, she didn't show it. She told me, 'Well, I'll more than likely be in. But if I'm not, I'll leave a note. And you do have your key.'

Then she was off. I watched her clopping down the path to the gate in her new shoes. 'Watch yourself, Mum,' I muttered at her stupidly high heels as she got in the car. 'Don't forget every single thing you say or do might end up in the notebook that you gave me.'

Some ancient great-aunt

I'd wanted to get to school early. The run-in I'd had with Jake had broken down some barrier between us. I'd got on with him well enough before – but just as one more boy who's always been in the same year and sometimes in the same class. We'd never had any particular contact. But now it was as if we'd somehow become friends.

And there was something that I wanted to know.

I tracked him down to the bike shed, where he was trying to snap his padlock shut. 'Jake?'

He glanced up. 'Hi, Scarlet.'

I forced myself to stop pawing the ground in embarrassment. 'Can I ask you something about your uncle?'

He was still struggling with the padlock. 'I should have oiled this thing. Well, fire ahead.'

'Is he rich?'

That startled Jake. 'Is he *rich*? Why do you ask that?'

'Our house,' I said. 'The one he sorted out. It's actually really nice, on a wide leafy street and with big sunny rooms. I know my parents can't have shared everything out yet. So I was just wondering how . . .'

Not knowing how to finish, I dried up. But I had obviously said enough because he finally jammed the padlock shut and said, 'Oh, I know about that! Mum told me. There was some ancient great-aunt somewhere in the family who always really liked him. She had a flat in London and Uncle Richard went round there a lot.'

I can't say I was keen to hear anything nice about his uncle. 'Was that because he knew she was rich?'

If he'd said something that catty about a favourite uncle of mine, I'd have clammed up at once. But Jake kept chatting as we left the shed and walked across the courtyard. 'Well, Dad jokes that it was just to cadge a free bed whenever he was in London. But Mum says that's not fair, and Richard was very good to Great-aunt Daisy. She says he sat with her for hours when she was dying in the hospital.'

We'd reached the double doors. I knew Jake wouldn't want to stand there talking for too long, or everyone who passed would get the wrong idea and start to tease us.

'Anyhow,' he said, 'Daisy left him the flat. He sold it for a packet.'

'And that's how he's helping my mum?'

'Must be. All I know is what Mum told me – that he's used most of the money to buy a house on Barlow Street. With what was left over he bought some very cheap flat behind the railway station. He plans to do that up and rent it out.'

'Thanks, Jake,' I said. 'Thanks.' I turned away. Our new house is on Barlow Street. And that disgusting flat we moved to first was by the railway station. So Richard Naylor's money had made Mum's move from our old home as easy-peasy, problem-free as packing a few boxes and choosing the day.

I reckoned, if it hadn't been for Great-aunt Daisy's generosity, my mother might still be at home with Dad.

'Fess up!'

When we were going to our sets for Maths, Bicky pranced up beside me. 'Hi, Scarlet. So what's the news? Fess up!'

At first I thought she must have seen me talking to Jake before the bell rang. I tried to fob her off. ''Fess up about *what*?'

'This boyfriend of your mum's, of course.' She grinned

as if my whole life was some stupid pantomime. 'You've met him, haven't you?'

'No,' I said fairly coldly. Then, like an idiot, I added, 'My mum hasn't brought him home yet.'

Bicky made one of her faces. 'Why wouldn't she do that?'

'How should I know?' I could have added what I thought, which was, 'It might be guilt. Or even embarrassment.' But none of it was Bicky's business. I hoped she'd prance off further down the corridor to bother someone else. But I was out of luck because it just so happened that Jake was behind us with a couple of mates.

Bicky swung round. 'Jake? Scarlet and I want to know all about your uncle.'

'*I* don't!' I snarled at her. But Bicky wasn't going to let me spoil her fun. 'Come on, Jake. Ignore grumpy Scarlet. Broadcast the newsflash. What's he like?'

Jake looked almost as embarrassed as I felt. 'What do you mean, what's he like?'

'You know,' said Bicky. She made her eyes go huge. (I think she thinks it looks sexy.) 'Start with the basics. Is he good-looking?'

Jake shrugged a sort of apology towards me, and said, 'I think so. Well, Mum says he is.'

'And is he *nice*?'

Jake tried to tease his way out of it. 'Bicky, his second

71

name is Naylor. So how could he be anything but clever and charming?'

Bicky was giggling. To her, the whole thing was a joke. 'Like you, you mean?'

'Like me.'

She pounced. 'So why won't Scarlet's mum let Scarlet meet him?'

'Won't she?' Startled, Jake looked at me. And I've no doubt that he could see that I was absolutely cringing with shame and fury. If Dr Chohan hadn't been only a few steps behind, I would have given Bicky such a push that she'd have fallen over.

Jake tried to make things easier with a smart remark. 'I expect that she wants to keep him all to herself. My aunt Maria always says he's the best-looking man in the family. Apart from me, of course.'

'But what about his personality?'

Jake was still eyeing me. We all find Bicky's teasing over the top, but he could tell she was upsetting me. He told her gravely, 'All I can tell you is that he's a really nice uncle.'

Bicky had moved in front of all of us now. She was dancing backwards. 'So he'll make a really good father?'

I snapped, 'I have a dad already, thanks!' and turned away, waiting for Alice to rescue me by catching up.

Bicky gave up and danced ahead.

Jake shrugged. 'Don't be too mad at her. I don't think she was thinking about *you*.'

I stood there, horrified, as Jake took off towards his own Maths room. Till he'd said that, it hadn't once occurred to me – not for a single moment – that Mum was young enough to have another baby.

But it did now.

'God! Not your *mum*?'

If Mum was in her late twenties when she had me, and I'd just had my birthday . . .

I caught Alice by the arm and whispered, 'How old can you be, and still have babies?'

She'd missed the conversation in the corridor, so she had no idea what I was on about. 'What?'

'Having a *baby*. What is the latest sort of age that someone can have one? How old might you be?'

She stared at me, appalled. 'God! Not your *mum*?'

Another friend who thought that it was possible! 'I was just *asking*.'

We were outside our own Maths room now, and guessing that Miss Harper was about to call to us, Alice pulled me inside. 'I know that fifty's iffy,' she was whispering as we threaded our way to our places. 'I think it's really rare to have them at that age.'

'But my mum's nowhere near as old as that.'

Miss Harper lost patience. 'Scarlet! Alice! Choose desks apart today, and that'll save me from having to move one or another of you later.'

So I was stuck there for an hour or more, not following a thing Miss Harper said, or anything on the board. All I could think of was the things you read and see about women having babies. My head swam with weird images of Mum waddling around the town with a huge swollen belly, or wearing one of those huge, ugly bras with extra flaps and hooks. I'd seen enough on telly to know the father's almost always in the room during the birth. And I knew what that looked like – not at all pretty, and nothing I would like a man who's not my dad to see. No, not if it was my mother with her nightie rucked up on the hospital bed.

I kept on telling myself, 'Get a grip, Scarlet! The only reason that you're in a stew is because Bicky set off a stupid train of thought. It's nothing to do with real life. Your mum's not going to have a baby. That man is not about to be your stepfather, and you're not going to have a little half-brother or sister to keep you awake all night.'

Except I knew that it was possible. Motty's mum had a baby only last year. I'd seen her with the buggy outside the school gates. I'd walked past Helena's father's car and seen a toddler strapped in its safety seat. That would be Helena's half-brother. And Pedro reckons that it's only a matter of time before this new stepfather of his persuades his mum to go broody.

'And if the circle has a radius of three point five?'

Miss Harper was looking at me. I hadn't got the faintest idea what she was talking about, let alone what she'd asked me. And Alice was two rows in front.

Beside me, hidden by Tom's back, Marina scribbled '*same*' and pointed with her finger.

'The same?' I said.

'Exactly!' said Miss Harper. She seemed quite pleased with me. 'See how much better you and Alice concentrate, when you are sitting apart?' She pedalled on for a while about coordinates. I wasn't listening. It was another load of stuff I knew I'd have to take home and try to work out on my own before the Tuesday lesson.

But I could do that Monday night. The job would keep me safe upstairs, away from Mum. And that was just as well, because I was as furious with her as if she had been pregnant for the last nine months, and had just given birth to triplets or quads.

Too deep for tears

I don't suppose Dad realized what had hit him. There he was, peacefully leaning over the bonnet of his car to polish the smears off his windscreen, when I turned up and started in on him. 'Why is there only me?'

'Sorry?'

'You heard. And you know what I'm asking too. Why is there only *me*?' Wrenching the car door open, I perched on the passenger seat at the front. 'Come on, Dad. I've asked you *loads* of times. You've always make a joke of it. Rubbish, like, "How could we ever have even dreamed of getting *another* angel?" But now I want to know the real truth. Why is there only me?'

He turned all shifty. 'What's brought this on, Scarlet?'

I glowered at him. 'Dad, I'm not a small child. I have a right to know what's going to happen. I want to know if Mum might have a baby with this Richard Naylor bloke.'

'Oh dear.'

I'd been expecting him to say, 'A *baby*?' In fact, I'd been expecting him to be as startled at the very idea as I had been.

But clearly not. For just the way he sighed, 'Oh dear',

made it quite plain he'd guessed this conversation might be on the cards. He still looked horribly uncomfortable, and tried one more bolt hole. 'Scarlet, sweetie, don't you think that your mother is the one you ought to ask about this?'

'Don't try that one,' I warned. 'She isn't *here*. She *left*. So I am asking *you*. And don't try fobbing me off, because I'm not a tennis ball to be bounced back and forth between the two of you, just because neither of you has the guts to tell me the truth.'

I watched him think about this. I even saw his hand making a move towards the pocket in which he keeps his phone, as if he had decided to ring Mum. But almost instantly he drew it back. 'I'll tell you this much, Scarlet. Unless your mother decides to adopt, I truly doubt if you will have any new brothers or sisters.'

'Why's that? People in class say that she's not too old.'

Now he looked really shocked. 'You haven't been discussing this at school!'

'No. I just asked how old was too old to have babies. And Mum's not there yet.'

'No, not yet. Not by a long shot.' He reached past me to pick up the crumpled garage worksheet that had been lying about in the car since its last service. I thought for a moment he was about to change the subject – start in about how soon the car was going to need new tyres, or brake linings, or something. But no. Without even noticing what he was doing, he started to fold the worksheet into narrow strips. 'Still, I think I can tell you, Scarlet, that it's not going to happen.'

'Why not?'

His voice, quite suddenly, didn't sound like his. 'Because she tried for years and years. And you were the only luck we had.'

I've learned enough biology to know there might have been lots of reasons for that. I didn't want to get Dad more upset than he was already. Still, I had to ask. 'But maybe, if she's trying with someone else . . . ?'

He shook his head. 'No, Scarlet. It would be the same problem.'

I wasn't going to let up. Why should I? 'So what problem's that?'

He took a deep breath. Perhaps he reckoned he was in so far he might as well tell the whole story. Tearing the worksheet into strips, along one fold after another, he said, 'Your mother is a most unlucky woman in that respect. Something about the way she's built makes it almost impossible for her to keep a baby going long enough.'

'She managed with me.'

'Yes, thankfully she managed with you. But you were the only one who made it.'

'So there were others?' My head was spinning. 'Were they before, or after?'

'Both.' He was staring at the ground. 'But tears ran too deep, and we agreed to give up.'

Tears ran too deep? I'd never heard my father say *anything* like that. In fact, I'd never even seen him pick up a poetry book. The Valentines that he gave Mum were mostly jokey ones. It was as if he were a different person suddenly.

I had just one more question. 'Does Richard Naylor know?'

There was the longest silence. He looked at the fan of paper strips he'd torn off the garage worksheet and swallowed hard. Again, his voice sounded different, a bit choked, when finally he answered.

'I have to say, I hope for his sake that he does.'

'Give your old man a break. Pretend you're still four.'

Dad seemed a little nervous after that. I saw him eyeing me more than once with the most baffled look, as if he'd never seen my face before and was confused to find a stranger in his house. It got a bit unsettling after a while, so the next time I caught him at it, I stretched out my hand and said sarcastically, 'Hi! Very pleased to meet you, Mr Warner. I'm Scarlet, and I'm your daughter.'

He took the point. 'Sorry,' he said. 'It's just that I'm a little dazed by that conversation we had.'

I didn't see why I should have to defend myself. Still, I said stubbornly, 'I had a right to know.'

He reached out to pat my hand. 'Yes, Scarlet. I think you did. But maybe I should have checked with your mother first?' He left this idea hanging in the air for only a moment before dismissing it. 'Though I suppose that, now she's gone, I can't keep checking with her about everything.'

How wet can your father get? 'No. No, you can't.'

'It's just that all that stuff seemed . . .'

Once again, he stopped.

I was exasperated. 'What?' I snapped. 'Private? Personal? Nosy?'

He found the words. 'Grown-up.'

'Grown-*up*?'

'Yes,' he said. 'Grown-up. *Horribly* grown-up.'

I liked the 'horribly'. For the first time in the whole conversation, I gave him a bit of a smile. 'I'm only one day older than I was yesterday, I promise.'

That made him laugh. He pulled me down beside him on the sofa. 'Oh, come on, Scarlet. Give your old man a break. Pretend you're still four, and come and sit on my knee.'

I snuggled up beside him for a while. When I got bored, I reached for the Spice Island take-out curry list on the fat sofa arm and folded it into a concertina. He took it and pretended to play, making a stupid wheezing noise. Then suddenly he said, 'Scarlet, you're right about this place. It's getting to look a real dump.'

'That's not quite what I said. It's not *that* bad.'

'Yes, it is.' He pointed to the wall in front of us. 'Before you mentioned all those patches, I hadn't noticed them. But now they're getting on my nerves. As for that stupid shower curtain I bought to replace the red one . . .'

'You should have looked at it more carefully before you bought it.'

He grunted. 'How was I supposed to know, simply from seeing it in the packet, that it was going to spend its whole life trying to stick to my bum?'

'It's not the little men in rockets bothering you?'

'What little men in rockets?'

'Haven't you even *looked* at it?'

He stared at me for a moment. Then he became a different man. 'Put your shoes back on, Scarlet. You and I are going shopping.'

'Charity shops aren't open this late,' I warned him.

'We're going to that mall at Hatcher's Cross. Most places there don't close till nine. We're going to buy a proper shower curtain. And some *paint*.'

I couldn't get my shoes on fast enough.

Alarm bells!

We drove to one of the giant places just off the bypass. On the way, I asked, 'Can I pick the colours?'

'*One* colour, Scarlet. This isn't going to be a teenage squat.'

'Promise me you won't go for boring old cream or magnolia.'

'I promise *nothing*.'

The moment we were in the paint aisle, Dad stopped sounding quite so masterful. 'Are these *all* colour charts? But there are dozens of them! How in heaven's name is anyone supposed to *choose*?'

'They ask their daughter, of course.'

He snorted. But we soon got down to it, dismissing some of the strips of colours out of hand ('No purples, thank you.') but keeping others in mind. We'd only just begun to niggle over our separate favourites when someone strolled up the aisle and stopped beside us. 'Is there any way I could help you? Would you like some advice?'

I thought she had a bit of a cheek, breaking in like that on two people arguing perfectly happily. But then I saw that she was wearing the official store shirt and had a name badge. It said *Laura Deloy*. If I had been with Alice, I think we would have told her we were managing fine all on our own, thanks. But I was with Dad. And maybe because this shop lady looked a bit like Henry Maddox's amiable, easy-going wife next door, Dad didn't make up some polite excuse to shoo her away.

Alarm bells! After a minute or two, it was quite obvious that he was warming to her. And I thought I knew why. It was because she disapproved of every single colour I suggested. Not all that gently, either. She kept on saying things like, 'Oh no, dear! That sort of fighting shade won't go with *anything*,' and, 'You like *that*? Really? We only usually sell colours this bright to children's play centres.'

But I do have to admit that she was fair. She wouldn't stand for anything Dad fancied either. 'No, no! On a wall, that'll look nothing short of *muddy*,' and, 'Oh, yes. It's pleasant enough. But it is *far* too dull! Surely you want to keep your living room looking *alive*?'

We were there nearly half an hour, and in the end we settled for a nice warm grey with pinky overtones. Even then, Laura Deloy had her doubts. 'I admit it's a safe shade,' she told us. 'Maybe almost *too* safe. But at least it's a colour that knows how to share with a few cheery extras.'

I had to tell Dad what that meant. 'She means that it'll go with lamps and cushions and ornaments and stuff.'

She waved us off to choose the cheery extras by ourselves. We dumped the paint cans in the car, then ambled back and, in no time at all, without her help, we bought a multi-coloured zigzag rug, some photo frames and four bright patterned plant pots.

Triumph!

When we got home, I helped Dad stack the cans and bags and boxes in the space where Mum's computer desk had been before she took it away. 'Are we starting tonight?'

'No, we are not,' Dad told me. 'I'm tired and hungry, and it's getting late.'

We tossed for what to have, and pizza won. We didn't make a salad. 'I'm going to have to get my act together,' Dad admitted as we sat together, munching. 'You and I cannot live on take-outs and frozen meals for ever.'

'I wouldn't mind.'

Before, he always would have said, 'I don't doubt that! But I'm afraid your mother would.'

This time he simply took the last slice of pizza that I waved away and said, 'No doubt.'

I hid my smile. But I did reckon I was making headway at last, training my dad to be a single parent.

Changing a few things round

I wasn't at Mum's house for three whole nights, and when I did get back, she'd pushed the boat out. Supper was one of my favourites – her home-made rogan josh curry swimming in tomatoes. She knows I love it.

I'd guessed she wouldn't be able to get through the meal without asking me a heap of questions about my time at Dad's. And sure enough, almost as soon as she'd finished dishing up, she started working her way towards the subject by saying as casually as she could, 'I think I was expecting you to come back here last night.'

I noticed she was playing safe by calling where we were 'back here', not pushing her luck by using the word 'home'. But I was still on guard.

'I left a message.'

'Oh, yes. You did the right thing and you let me know.' Then, without even asking me about what I'd been up to at school, or with Alice, in the last couple of days, she took another tack to try to get to what she wanted to know. 'Your dad was well, was he?'

So there you go. Between one mouthful and the next I

was annoyed with her. It was the *nerve* of it! It seems to me the parent who walks out has no right to have it both ways. If you want to know all about what's going on with your old husband, then you ought to stay with him.

That is the only reason I started to torment her. 'Oh, there was nothing wrong with him,' I told her cheerfully. 'It's just that we were really busy changing a few things round.'

I could tell Mum was dying to ask me what I meant. But before she could even open her mouth, I swept on, telling her about some silly thing that happened in my English class that morning, and then, at enormous, boring length, about what Alice and her family had done over the weekend. I just kept talking and talking. Mum didn't dare to try to interrupt to drag me back to what I'd been up to with Dad. It would have looked too prying and too obvious. So she made a huge effort to pretend to take an interest in Alice's grandmother's sixtieth birthday party walk over the hills, and all the stuff I told her about school.

And luckily, just as I was flagging (and my curry was getting cold), her phone rang.

It was the hospital, in one of their usual panics. She ran upstairs to find the paperwork she needed, and while she was busy with the call I bolted down the rest of my supper and went about my job of stacking the dishwasher. I wiped down the table and the counters as fast as I could, and managed to get the whole lot done before she was finished on the phone. I didn't see why I should hang around to face more questions and risk spoiling my fun. So, waving at her cheerily as I squeezed by, I fled upstairs.

'Laura?'

I knew – just knew – that she'd been in my room. Maybe it wasn't quite as stuffy as I'd expected it to be after three days. Maybe something had been moved. I hadn't lived in the room long enough to be quite sure that I remembered properly where I had put the few things that I'd taken out of boxes. But I still knew she'd been in there.

Had she been looking for the scarlet book? She'd have been disappointed, then. It was nowhere she'd find it. Still, it was horrible to know almost for certain that I'd been right all along, and with her so-called 'gift' she had been hoping to keep tabs on what was in my mind. Either the most important thing to her was making life easy for me, in which case she should have stayed with Dad. Or being with her precious Richard Naylor mattered more, and she should stop trying to poke her nose into my feelings.

That's what I thought. So when she finally got up the nerve to ask me more about my weekend with Dad, I was so

87

furious with her, I did what I felt she'd just done to me and laid a trap.

Mine wasn't like hers. I wasn't trying to find out what was in her mind. I was putting something in it. 'Oh,' I said cheerfully. 'We just did up the living room. We reckoned it was a bit dingy the way it was. Both of us felt like a change.'

Even as I was coming out with it, I realized that it sounded odd, as if, instead of being father and daughter, Dad and I had turned into a team. I could tell Mum was startled. She did as good a job as she could to hide her surprise. 'So the two of you decided to shift things around a bit?'

'We did a lot more than that. We decorated it.'

'Really? What, with new wallpaper?'

'No. We decided not to go for wallpaper. So we used what was there as lining paper, and covered it over.'

'With paint?'

I gave her a cool stare. 'Yes, Mum. With paint.'

I could tell she was dying to ask more. And I was dying to carry on with what I wanted to say. But I knew it would seem more natural if I held out. And so I waited.

I watched Mum try to leave it. I could almost see her willing herself to drop the subject. But in the end, of course, her curiosity won out. She had to ask. 'So what colour did you paint it?'

Dancing towards the door, I called back airily over my

shoulder, 'Oh, don't ask me! I can't remember what it's called. Paint colours have such weird names. But it was a really good choice. Dad and I think it's made all the difference and the room looks amazing now.'

Out of pure spite, I tried to make it sound as if we'd thought the room looked terrible before.

Mum said unhappily, 'Well, even paint can work out quite expensive. It's lucky that the two of you are happy with the result.'

This was the chance that I'd been waiting for. 'I don't think it was *luck*,' I said. 'We had a lot of help from Laura.'

'Laura?'

But I had left the room.

'Richard!'

Of course, it turned out that I'd left the only Maths book I can understand over at Dad's. Mum offered to drive me there. I knew that was because she was so keen to see the changes to the house, so I said that I'd walk as far as Alice's and borrow her bike.

'But, Scarlet, that's silly. The trip will take five minutes in the car.'

'I feel like biking.'

'You know that I don't like you on that road when every-one's driving home.'

'I'll go the long way, along the cycle path around the park. After I'm off that, none of the roads are busy.'

'Why don't we just nip over now?' Already she was pick-ing up the car keys.

There was a knock on the door. I think we both guessed straightaway that it was Richard Naylor. Mum hesitated. I even wondered if she was going to signal me to stay quite still until whoever it was gave up and went away. But then she got a grip on herself, and opened the door.

'Richard!'

He leaned towards her. He was going to take her in his arms. Then he saw me, and changed his mind. 'Hi, Frances.' He looked at me a little nervously over her shoulder. 'I hope I haven't come at a bad time.'

I think he realized that he hadn't really said the right thing. So he pressed on. 'Is this your daughter? Yes! Of course it is.' He turned to me. 'You have to be Scarlet. You look so like your mother.'

Nobody takes to people who say things like that. I gave him quite a beady look.

Mum prompted, 'Scarlet?'

'Hello,' I said, but it was not the warmest greeting.

That's when he saw the car keys in Mum's hand. 'You were off out?'

'Not really, no,' Mum said. 'We were just nipping back to Scarlet's dad's house to pick up something she needs.'

Scarlet's dad's house! What was she talking about? She still owned half of it! She'd only just moved out! I was so cross, I said, 'Yes. We were just going back to Mum's other house to get my Maths book.'

That irritated Mum enough for her to say, 'But come in, Richard. I'm delighted you've dropped by. I'll make us all a cup of tea. Scarlet's homework can wait for half an hour.'

'It can't,' I said. 'I didn't understand any of the lesson. Sorting it out is going to take me ages.'

'What was the lesson about?' he asked me.

'Something to do with coordinates,' I told him sullenly. 'I've a whole worksheet of questions up in my room and no idea what I'm supposed to be doing.'

I only told him that much so Mum would feel awful about making me wait while she sat with her boyfriend drinking tea. Mistake! I'd said entirely the wrong thing.

'Bring down the paper,' Richard Naylor said. 'I'm an accountant. I'm spot-on at Maths. I can explain it.'

Oh, that was lucky. (Not!)

'Sit here, won't you?'

I looked at Mum. Mum looked at me.

I was the one who cracked. I went and fetched the worksheet.

I don't know what I'd been hoping Richard Naylor would be like (apart from a million miles away). But on the way up to my room, I had to admit to myself that he didn't look too awful, and I could see how someone Mum's age might be attracted to him. He had the same slanty green eyes and crinkled smile as Jonty Pepper, the stand-up comedian. When I came down, he took the worksheet from me, and without another word to either me or Mum, he flattened it on the table and studied it while Mum made all of us a cup of tea.

Then he reached out and pulled an empty chair around the table till it was right beside him. 'Sit here, won't you?'

I didn't see how I could argue. Mum was still watching me.

He started off. He didn't go at it at all like Miss Harper does, or even call things by the same names. But I still followed what he said. He did the first two by himself, talking me through them as he wrote down the working. Twice, as he did the next two, he suddenly broke off and waited for me to tell him what he should be putting down next. And when, the second time, I got it wrong, he managed to explain why in a way that made me understand better what we were supposed to be doing.

I did the next four questions by myself while he was chatting to Mum about some problem he'd had while he was trying to renew his passport. At one point, while he was right in the middle of explaining how he'd not filled in some form exactly right, his finger dropped on something I'd just written.

He hadn't even broken off talking to Mum – just pointed with his finger.

I looked again. It was a careless mistake and so I changed it, wondering how anyone could be so good at Maths that they could do a problem like that in their head – and get it right – while at the same time chatting about something else.

When I got to the bottom of the worksheet, he took it back and rubbed out both the answers he'd done for me right at the start.

He pushed it back towards me. 'Nearly done.'

I did those too.

'You're quick,' he told me. 'If I'd been doing this with Jake, we'd have been here for ages.'

I couldn't help it, I was curious. 'Do you help Jake with homework?'

'All the time.'

He gave me one of those wide, crinkly smiles. And suddenly the last thing that I wanted was for my mum to come out with, 'Scarlet, thank Richard for helping you,' as if I was some child.

So I said very quickly, 'Well, thanks for helping me.'

'Any time.'

He gave my mum a quick peck on the cheek, and left.

'No, not so lucky for him.'

I reckon Alice must have asked a million questions.

'So what does he look like?'

'I *told* you. Just like that Jonty guy you had a thing about.'

'But older, right?'

'Not that much older.'

She thought about it. 'Doesn't that make him a little bit young to be going around with your mum?'

'Not really, no. I mean, my mum's beginning to look younger herself. She wears her nicest clothes more often. And puts on lipstick and stuff.'

'So do they sort of fit together?'

'What do you mean?'

'Do they look right?'

'How should I know?' I asked her. 'Like I said, he just sat

there explaining how to do Miss Harper's homework, then watched me finish it. And then he left.'

'Just like that?'

'Just like that.'

'Was your mum disappointed that he went so soon?'

'I think she was just pleased I'd been polite.'

'Thanking him properly, and all that?'

'Yes.'

Alice was thrilled. 'If Richard Naylor's anywhere near as good-looking as Jonty Pepper, then I can see why your mum fell for him. And he's nice too?'

'Yes,' I admitted. 'He is nice. And he is really, *really* good at Maths.'

'Lucky for you,' said Alice. She made a face. 'But not so lucky for your dad.'

'No, not so lucky for him.'

I had been wondering about that. I think, till I met him, I'd been hoping Richard Naylor would turn out horrible. Ugly and rude. Or stupid. Boring. Or fussy. Anything awful, really, so Mum might look at him one day quite soon and think to herself, Actually, I don't like this man nearly as much as I thought I did. I actually prefer Scarlet's dad.

It was as if Alice could read my mind. 'So your mum won't be rushing back home any time in the near future?'

I didn't have to answer that because our darling Archie rolled over and woke up.

Archie

Archie is Alice's baby cousin. Whenever her aunt Bev comes round to see her sister, we kidnap him and carry him upstairs. He's only one, so still takes naps, and when he falls asleep we dump him down on Alice's bed. One of us has to stay close, to keep him from falling off because he's what Bev calls 'a thrasher'. He moves about so much when he's asleep that he can end up the wrong way round and back to front, and never once wake up unless he falls on the floor.

I adore Archie. I love everything about him. When he was tiny, he only used to sleep and eat and fill his nappies. I didn't even mind taking a turn at changing those. It was more interesting than disgusting because it was always different. Sometimes it looked as if he had dropped hard dark-brown pebbles into his nappy. Sometimes it was more like a squidgy fudge, all moulded to his bottom. Sometimes it was squittery. Whatever he produced came out all sorts of shades of brown and yellow, but never smelled too bad, and there was something really cheering about cleaning him up, and pinning down his wriggles to wrap his small pink bottom safely in another clean and dry, fresh-smelling nappy.

Now Archie's almost walking. When he's awake, he staggers along the edge of the bed, clinging to Alice's duvet. (One of us has to stay on the bed even then, so that the duvet doesn't get tugged off onto the floor.)

And he's beginning to talk. The only things that he can say so far are 'Ma', which sometimes means Bev and sometimes milk. You have to work out for yourself which one he wants. (Until Bev gave up breast feeding after his birthday, it usually used to mean both.) And he has also taken to saying, 'Der-yar.' We couldn't work out what he meant by that for quite a while, until I noticed that, whenever he was saying it, he had some sort of toy or biscuit in his hand and he was thrusting it our way.

We told Bev, 'Archie's saying, "There you are."'

'Nonsense,' she said. 'How can he be? Archie can barely say "Ma".'

Alice's mother hadn't believed us either. 'And even then, he gets the word mixed up with "milk".'

'Well, he can say it,' we insisted. 'You listen, and you'll see.'

So they did start to listen, and after half an afternoon they had to admit we were right. Archie kept trying to stuff his toys in the dog's mouth. 'Der-yar.' He tried to shove a biscuit into mine. 'Der-yar!' He tried to give Alice a spoonful of the milky mush he eats before his nap. 'Der-yar!'

'Isn't he *clever*!' Bev crowed. 'A three-word sentence, and he's only just turned one.'

'It isn't a three-word sentence,' Alice's father had argued. 'Not to Archie. Not if he doesn't realize that it is. Which he most certainly doesn't.'

But Alice's mother took our side, and off they'd gone, all through the meal, arguing the way they do. Alice and I had been sitting one on either side of the high chair, spooning mush into Archie, saying, 'Der-yar!' every other time, and 'There you are,' very clearly every time in between, till Mr Henty told us both that it was getting tiresome and we were to knock it off.

But this particular time, Archie had woken in the grumpiest mood and it took all our efforts to keep him happy. So it was only later, when Bev had taken him off and I was borrowing Alice's bike to go back to my mum's place, that she had tugged at my arm. 'Honest answer? Whatever?'

She often starts our conversations this way.

'All right,' I told her. 'Honest answer. Whatever.'

She put the question. 'If your mum wasn't already going out with his uncle, would you have maybe gone a bit soft on Jake?'

I stared at her. 'No way!'

She had a not-quite-sure-that-I-believe-you look on her face.

'No way!' I said again. 'Not on this planet!'

I don't think that I've ever biked away so fast.

Texting and sexting

How do you open the most beautiful notebook you've ever seen, and start to write in it, when you don't even know what you think? I wasn't even sure what I *felt*. I must have sat there on the window seat until my hand was sticky, holding my fine-tipped pen over the first thick, creamy page. So many excellent first sentences ran through my brain. 'My mother's the most selfish person on the *planet*.' 'My mum's an *idiot*.' 'My mother has just spoiled my life, my dad's, and – I really, really hope – her own.'

But none of them was absolutely right. I couldn't be sure I wouldn't want to cross them out to start again, spoiling the shiny scarlet book for ever.

I wondered for a moment whether to give up on my plan to use the book to upset Mum, and keep it for myself. And that, of course, immediately set me thinking about the other things that I might write about.

School? Alice?

Jake?

I wasn't miffed with Alice for hinting that he and I might end up more than friends. I thought, if anything, that she was trying to be nice. Still, what she'd said did spook me. Some of the people in our class have started fancying other people – even hanging out with them. But I am used to thinking of that gang as being different from Alice and me.

We tease them. 'There you go again. Texting and sexting.'

'We are not sexting!'

'Prove it. Show us.'

'Get lost. Mind your own business. What age are you, anyway? Five?'

If you go looking, you can see the most amazing pictures of some of the girls in our class. You know that they don't really look like that because you see them every day. You know they must have spent hours and hours getting the pose and the face and the clothes right. I showed my dad Marina's photo once, with all its thumbs-up Likes. He stared at it for a while. 'This girl is actually in your *class*? She's *your* age, Scarlet?'

'Actually, Marina's two months younger than me.'

'Frogs' knickers!'

(Don't even ask. I think it's probably the only thing his mother – that's Our Lady of the Turned-out Lavatory Rolls – ever allowed him to say.)

He kept on peering closely at the screen, like some detective inspecting the photo of a victim's corpse.

'Da-ad!' I said. 'This is getting rather pervy!'

Hastily he handed back the phone. 'Well!' he said, shaking his head in amazement. 'I probably sound like a dinosaur to you, but all I can tell you is that if any girl in my school had gone around as good as saying, "Here is a beautiful photo of me! Do you like it?" she'd have been sent to have her temperature taken.' He thought for a while, then added, 'And if a boy had done it, I think that probably the rest of us would have queued up to biff some sense into him.'

I love my dad when he says old-fashioned things like that. It makes it so much easier not to be bothered by all the people in our school who go round thumbing and liking and favouriting and friending and checking and scrolling and tapping and following and ghosting and whatever.

Alice's parents go practically unhinged whenever the subject comes up. It's almost the only thing that they agree on. I've heard her mum go on about it so often. 'Those things just offer you poor girls a million extra ways to feel like rubbish. In my day, if we left someone out, that's all we did. We left them out. Most of the time, they wouldn't even know that they'd not been invited. Now everyone beats the jungle drum, with added photographs to ram the message home.' She apes a silly voice. '*Look! Here's a good one of me trying on skimpy dresses in Topshop with Beth and Amy! Just them, mind. You might have thought you were our friend, but you're not here, are you? You didn't even know that we were going! But you do now!*' Or, '*Don't miss this! See?*

Belinda and I have gone to Pizza Express and you're not in the photo! You didn't get to come!'

Her dad gets even more grumpy on the topic. 'All these "having a great time" and "look at my new top" and "see my beautifully made-up face" photos flashing about. It's just a trick to make you want to grow up faster so that you'll buy more stuff. You shouldn't fall for it.'

Alice and I roll our eyes and keep a tight grip on our phones. But I know that there's something real in what he says. Marina has three whole clothes drawers full of all the make-up and hair stuff that she's bought over the last couple of years. Yet, for all that she has a slew of lovely, smiling photos staring out, it's not as if she's happy inside. She's always wondering what people think of her. She stays up half the night checking her phone. She says that if she switches off she just feels anxious, worrying she might be missing something.

'*Not* a good use of your time,' Tom Wilcox scolded her once.

She nearly spat at him. I was astonished. Marina and I have known one another ever since primary school. I never would have thought she could turn out so tense and ratty. I'd hate to end up worrying, the way Marina does now, about how she comes across to everyone – even to people who don't even know her. I would hate that so much.

Still, Alice had rattled me with what she'd said about me

and Jake. My mum has always said that Alice pokes her nose in things too fast. But Alice is often right. And if she'd said what she did about, say, Philip – or Pedro or Greg – I'd have just laughed and reckoned she was being funny.

But Jake is lovely. I like him a lot.

Out by one

I'm not quite sure what made me hide the fact that all our year group had an afternoon off. Miss Sinton had droned on during Assembly about some problem with the boiler. I wasn't really listening. So it was only after we were back in our home room that I cottoned on, because the racket round me got louder and louder:

'Yes! Out by one tomorrow!'

'Ace! I'll be off to the mall with Bicky.'

'Good job my parents never read the posts from school. They'd find some way to ruin my afternoon.'

'Is *Vampire Quest* still showing? If so, that's me and Chris sorted.'

I gave Alice a nudge. 'What's everyone on about?'

She gave me a small push back. 'Weren't you even *listening*? The main boiler's being fixed. So everyone down our corridor gets off straight after lunch tomorrow.'

'Why?'

'Something to do with Health and Safety.' She shrugged. 'Who cares? Want to come round to my place?'

'*Please.*'

But when she asked her mum, that plan was shelved. 'Sorry, Scarlet. She wants me to go with her to Bev's to babysit Archie while she takes Bev for some check-up.'

'Can't I come with you?'

'I did ask, but she said the car will be crammed full of stuff for Bev's new flat.'

'Oh well. I'll think of something to do.'

She grinned. 'You'd better do that fast, before your mother thinks of something *for* you.'

So maybe it was that remark of Alice's that made me say nothing that night. Mum asked about my day. I told her as much as I would usually about the lessons, and the weirdly gritty salad at lunch, and Dr Deiss getting even more ratty than usual.

But I never once mentioned our free afternoon.

As she picked up her keys and work bag in the morning, she gave me the usual peck on the cheek. 'Be good. I'll see you after school. And if you get in first, try to remember to switch on the tumble dryer.'

'OK,' I told her. 'If I get in first.'

A few secret hours off

Of course I got in first. Like everyone else in our class, I'd pushed my way into first lunch sitting, and I was out of school by one. I was home even before the lunchtime news had finished on the radio that Mum leaves on in some vain hope that it might fool a burglar.

I switched the dryer on, then realized that if it ran through the cycle it would be finished well before Mum came home. That would cause trouble. 'Scarlet! You know I don't trust that dryer to run with no one in the house. I asked you to turn it on when you got back, not before you went off. Why don't you *listen*?'

So I put it on 'pause'. I mucked about for a while, watching some strange Welsh family kicking lumps out of one another on telly. I danced around to some of my favourite songs. I had a chat with Alice, till Archie squawked so loud she had to go. 'He keeps on grabbing the phone. I'm worried that he's going to knock it on the floor and break it. Talk later.'

I went upstairs and nosed through my mother's bedroom, looking for signs that Richard Naylor had been there. It was quite nice not to feel the slightest bit guilty as I slid my hand under her pillows, and checked the bedside cabinet and poked my fingers under the stuff in her jewellery basket. Hadn't she sneaked upstairs and snooped round my room for the scarlet book? Fair's fair, after all.

But I found nothing. In the end, I made a cup of the expensive hot chocolate we keep for treats, then had a long deep bath and washed my hair.

I was still towelling myself dry when the landline rang. I wasn't sure what to do. If Mum had somehow found out, quite by accident, that our year group had gone home early, she might be checking on me, using the house phone instead of mine so she could be quite sure I wasn't spinning her some story about my whereabouts.

She couldn't prove I hadn't honestly forgotten that school would end so early. I picked up the phone.

It was her secretary, Nadia.

'Fran?'

'No,' I admitted. 'This is Scarlet.'

She wasn't bothered. I am not her problem. 'Oh, Scarlet! I'm trying to track down your mum. Her phone's been going to the message bank all day, and Dr Claymore really needs advice about some grant application that's run up against its deadline. It's quite important.'

I knew enough about the hospital to ask, 'Why can't you page her?'

'Page her?'

'Why not?' I said. (Just about every time I've had to wait for Mum inside the hospital, I've heard staff being called by name to the white phones.)

'Your mum's not in today.'

'No?'

'No. Not today.'

I heard her speak to someone at her end. Then she came back to me. 'Scarlet, if she gets back, or even gets in touch, ask her to ring me. Tell her that it's important.'

'She should be back by half past four,' I said. 'Will that be soon enough?'

'I certainly hope so!'

'OK,' I said. 'I won't forget.'

I put the phone down. Peas in a pod, I thought. (That's what my other gran says every time she sees my mum and me standing together. 'Peas in a pod.')

I don't tell her I'm having a few secret hours off. And she does not tell me.

'Busy, was it? At the hospital?'

She came home at the usual time. Cool as a cucumber, she asked me, 'Did you remember to turn on the dryer?'

'I certainly did,' I said, all goody two-shoes, and turned away to take an apple from the bowl. 'Good day?'

'Not bad,' she said.

I turned to face her. 'Busy, was it? At the hospital?'

She shrugged. 'The usual. One stupid little emergency after another. A host of phone calls. Endless paperwork.'

Gotcha!

I moved in for the kill. 'You got it done, though? Dr Claymore's grant application?'

She stared at me. I took a giant crunch of apple in the way she hates.

'Dr Claymore's grant application,' I repeated before I'd even finished churning it around my mouth. 'You got that problem sorted?'

I knew how rattled she was because she didn't even take time out to tell me off for talking with my mouth full. 'Sorry, Scarlet?'

I shrugged, as if I hadn't even noticed that she'd been lying about her day. 'Nadia rang. About the grant deadline.'

'Oh, Christ!'

Without another word to me, Mum fled upstairs. I stayed in the kitchen. If anyone was watching through the window, they would have wondered what I was smirking about. But it felt wonderful to catch her out. She had been watching me so closely, and I was still mad at her for giving me the scarlet book.

It felt so good to know the tables had been turned.

She came back in the kitchen just as I flicked the switch to start on making her a pot of tea.

'Sorted?' I asked.

'All sorted. Yes.'

I could tell how relieved she was. Give her a chance, I thought, and for the second time since she'd come home, I asked, 'Good day?'

This time she told the truth. 'Yes,' she said. 'I took the whole day off. Richard and I went for a stroll along the viaduct. We had lunch at the Forester's Rest, and then strolled back.' She lifted two mugs off the shelf. 'It was a lovely walk. I don't believe I've been that way since you were a sweet little thing sitting bolt upright in your cute baby backpack, staring at everything!' She put the mugs beside the kettle and reached for the packet of tea bags. 'You and I ought to do it together again – maybe even this weekend?'

For heaven's sake! Was that what was filling her mind now? Notions of 'sweet little things sitting bolt upright in cute baby backpacks'? Pardon me while I throw up!

I hadn't pushed my luck. She shouldn't have pushed hers.

'Sorry,' I told her. 'I'll be at Dad's all this weekend. I think this time we're planning to redecorate the hall.'

'Sorry to burst in like this.'

I might have known that saying that would make Mum's curiosity about the changes in the other house boil over. But she was so sneaky about it. First, she asked if I'd be back at her place for supper on Sunday night. 'Just so I know if it's worth cooking something.'

I quite like having time to sort things out and pack for school. So, 'Fine,' I said. 'That'll be good.'

'By six at the latest? That way, your dad can drop you off and still get one of those really early nights he likes so much.'

'*Needs* so much,' I corrected in a sour mutter. But Mum pretended not to hear. And then she very cunningly didn't stick to the plan. On Sunday she showed up at half past four. When the doorbell rang, I could tell Dad was startled to see Mum waiting on the step – though I don't see how he could have imagined she might just fish out some old key and simply let herself in.

Still, the look on his face as he opened the door and she walked past him into the house was one of pure panic.

She sounded cheery enough. 'Sorry to burst in like this, but I was driving past and it occurred to me that I could save you the bother of giving Scarlet a lift back.' She stared round the freshly decorated hall. 'Nice!' she admitted. 'Very nice!'

'We've done the living room as well,' Dad told her, pushing open the door.

Now it was Mum's turn to be startled. 'Wow! That *is* a change!' She looked round at the new way we'd arranged the furniture. She nodded at the snazzy pots. She walked up closer to the photographs I'd chosen for the new frames and studied them for long enough to notice that they were all of me, or Dad, or me and Dad together. I felt bad when I saw her clocking that. I hadn't meant to make her feel that we'd been wiping her out of our lives. I'd just been trying to stop Dad moping over his memories of what was gone.

She managed something really generous. 'That's lovely, that one. And I have *always* liked that one of you and Scarlet on the swing.'

I helped her out. 'I tried to choose the photos where Dad still had a lot of hair.'

I felt the two of them relax a bit when I said that. Dad offered Mum some tea, and she said yes. I hurried out to make it, leaving Mum prowling round the room admiring the new zigzag rug and plant pots. I heard her say, 'I wish I'd thought to swap those chairs about, and have the telly over there instead.'

I left them to it while they drank their tea, and went upstairs to sort out what I needed to take back to the other house. They must have been discussing me because the tone of his voice changed as I came down again, and she interrupted whatever he was saying with a forceful, 'Yes, of course, Tony. I'll make sure I change the address on that.'

Putting her mug down, she asked me, 'Ready, Scarlet?'

I nodded. 'Ready.'

She turned to Dad. 'Well, I must say, I think the room looks lovely. You tell your Laura from me that I think she has done a brilliant job.'

She fled the house so fast she missed his look of total bafflement. And when the penny finally dropped, nor did she see the absolutely furious look that Dad gave me before I trailed out after.

'Told *who*? Told her *what*?'

'Pure, simple troublemaking!' That's what Dad called it next time I saw him.

I tried to defend myself. 'Her name *was* Laura. And she *was* very helpful. That's all I said. So how was I to know that Mum was going to think she was your girlfriend?'

He shook his head as if my explanation was so lame, so pitiful, that there was no point going on about the matter. It was the look you'd give a child of three who had been lying to you about eating sweets, or breaking a vase.

I wasn't going to put up with that, so I fought back. 'Oh, nice one, Dad! Stand around feebly watching your wife walk out, then take it out on me!'

I stormed out of the room.

It was some time before he called me down again on some excuse about the plan for supper. And even then I waited quite a while before I softened up enough to do anything more than answer his stupid questions about school as briefly as I could. So it was not until the pasta bake he'd made was out of the oven and onto the table that I thought it was safe to ask a question of my own. 'So have you *told* her?'

I could tell straightaway I'd jumped the gun, and he was still really irritated about the whole business. 'Told *who*? Told her *what*?'

'Told Mum. That Laura was just some sales lady we bumped into in the paint aisle.'

That's when I noticed that his face had gone a little red. 'Da-ad?'

He didn't answer – just sat there, probably pawing the floor tiles under the table in his embarrassment. It didn't take that long to work out what was running through his mind. 'You *fancied* her, didn't you? You want to see her again!'

'Scarlet, this isn't any business of yours at all.'

He'd got on his high horse so I got on mine. 'Oh, yes it is. I have to move between two places all the time. It's nice to know what's going on in them, and if I'm likely to bump into brand-new friends of yours as well as Mum's.'

'I don't think that's likely to happen.'

'Is that because you haven't seen this Laura again? Or because you haven't asked her here yet?' I knew I had my dad on the back foot, so took the chance to stop him being mad at me by starting on a tease. 'You ought to invite her – if only so she can see how right she was about the paint colour she bullied us into choosing.'

He grinned. 'Oh, come on, Scarlet. You couldn't really call it bullying.'

'She was rude about all my suggestions.' I pointed my fork at him. 'And some of yours.'

He made a face.

'Go on,' I ordered him. 'Fess up! Has she been here, or not?'

My dad was practically writhing with embarrassment. 'She did pop in once, yes. Last Wednesday afternoon.'

'Just to admire our handiwork? Not to see you?'

Now he was going red again. 'Well, possibly. A little. Who's to say?'

'You are,' I told him firmly. 'You're not a halfwit. Does this Laura Delilah—'

'Deloy.'

'Deloy. Does she stalk all her customers? Check out where they live, and come round making sure they did a

114

proper job? Or did you think of some excuse to go back to the mall to chat her up?'

'It wasn't an excuse. I needed wood protective for the back fence.'

'Which has been rotting happily for years.'

I gave him a few more moments to shift about uncomfortably, then, curious, I asked, 'So does this Laura Deloy fancy you back?'

His face took on a baffled look. 'I'm not sure. But I think she might quite like me. She stayed much longer than she would have needed just to see the room.'

'She wouldn't have come here just to see the room at all,' I told him. 'You know that. She doesn't have to make home visits. If she came round here, it's because she likes you.'

'Really?' he said. 'You truly think that?'

Honestly. The way he said it, you'd have thought that he was someone in my class and not my dad at all.

'Your parents!'

Of course I had to tell Alice. We'd been sent out with Archie. ('He needs fresh air,' said Mrs Henty, strapping him into the pushchair. 'And poor Bev needs an hour or two of peace.')

We went across the park, and while Archie shredded all the leaves we handed him, I explained about Laura.

'Your parents!' Alice said. 'It's getting to be as good as a soap opera.' She bumped Archie over a branch that lay across the path. 'You ought to write down every episode and sell it to telly.'

'It'd be far too volcanic for family viewing.'

'X-rated stuff? Well, I'll be happy to dump my library book the minute you're ready to share what you've got written in the scarlet book.'

'I've not even got going yet.'

Alice grinned. 'Pity.' As she reached down to offer Archie another leaf, she added, 'Is your mum still hunting for it, do you think?'

I shrugged. 'Not sure. I wouldn't be surprised. I mean, she comes upstairs to put my laundry on my bed often enough. Who's to say what she roots through when she's there?'

'Guess what my mum found under my bed when she was up in my room on the search for—'

I didn't get to hear what Mrs Henty had been looking for, or what she found, because just then there was the most enormous thunderclap.

Within a moment, rain was bucketing down.

'Your mum's house!' Alice said. 'Quick! Before we get soaked.'

We ran so fast that Archie thought it was a game. He howled when we reached the front porch and Alice unbuckled him. I let us in. Mum wasn't there. She'd been expecting me to stay at Alice's all afternoon. Alice calmed Archie down and peeled off his sodden jacket. She towelled his head dry while I turned the heating up and switched on the kettle. Then Archie crawled about on the floor of our living room, scraping up bits of fluff from our new carpet and putting little balls of the stuff into his nose.

'Don't do that,' Alice told him. 'It's disgusting! Stop it!'

'Do you think he understands when you say things like that?'

'He understands the word "No!". But I daren't say that as it makes him cry.' She sighed. 'Mum says that that's because, ever since Archie began teething, Bev's had so little sleep she's letting him get spoiled rotten.'

'That isn't fair. It can't be easy, having a baby all on your own. I think Bev's a really good mother.'

'So do I.'

We sat side by side on the floor with our backs against the sofa, sipping tea and lifting our mugs away from Archie's grabbing hands every few seconds. 'Do you remember what this Laura Deloy looked like?' asked Alice.

'Not really, no,' I said. 'I mean, I'm sure I'd recognize her in the shop because I'd be expecting to see her there. But if she passed me on the street, I'm not so sure.'

Alice said mischievously, 'Well, we could always go and buy some paint . . .'

'It's miles away, that place! At Hatcher's Cross.'

'We have bikes.'

'She might not be at work that day. We don't know anything at all about her schedule.'

'You could ask your dad.'

'No way!' I told her. 'Absolutely no way!'

'Absolutely no way *what*?'

We heard a cheery voice behind us. 'Absolutely no way *what*?'

I twisted round to look. Richard Naylor! He'd let himself in through the kitchen door and we'd not heard him over Archie's babbling.

I can't say I was pleased. Totally forgetting that he was the person who actually owned the house, I told him frostily, 'I didn't realize that you had a key.'

He almost fell over himself, apologizing. 'I'm sorry! Really sorry. I would have waited till your mum showed up, but I walked from the office and it's pelting down. Frances told me that she'd be back by three. I saw her car wasn't outside, but I'm afraid it never occurred to me that there'd be

anyone else here. She said you would be out all afternoon.'
He stepped a little further into the room, still talking. 'I'm
sorry if I startled you and' – now he was making a sort of
formal bow towards the sofa we were leaning against – 'and
Alice, is it?'

'Yes,' Alice said. 'I'm Alice. And this is Archie.'

Richard Naylor seemed to fold himself up in much the
same way as our ironing board. Before we knew it, he was
down at our level, sitting on the floor the other side of Archie.

Archie put his palms flat on the carpet and used his
arms as levers to upend his bottom. From there, he grabbed
at Alice's sleeve in order to keep steady while he pulled
himself upright. Then he reached out both arms like a small,
chubby zombie and staggered over to fall untidily in Richard
Naylor's lap.

'Sorry,' said Alice automatically. 'He does that.'

'So I see.'

Richard set Archie on his feet again. He staggered back
to Alice. Then Alice set him up and sent him over to me.

'Can he not walk yet, then?' asked Richard Naylor.

'Yes,' I said sarcastically. 'This is him doing it. This is
Archie walking.'

'I mean, proper distances.'

'What?' I asked. 'Like a country ramble? Or a half
marathon?'

He chuckled, as if I had said something really amusing.

And Alice laughed as well. I could tell that she liked him, and I admit that he was being perfectly easy and amiable with the three of us, there on the floor without Mum.

'Don't you know anything at all about toddlers?' Alice dared ask him.

'Not really, no.'

'You've never seen a baby before?'

'Not one as gorgeous as this.'

Alice jumped at the chance. 'But you're Jake's uncle. Surely you must have known Jake when he was this age?'

You could tell Richard Naylor was thinking back. 'I suppose I must. But Jake was nowhere near as cute as this little fellow.' As he was speaking, he reached out to press Archie's nose as if it were a buzzer, but very gently. 'Don't tell him I said this, but all I can remember about Jake as a baby is him lying in his cot, interminably grizzling. And forever having tantrums. Dribbling, of course. And spitting out his food. I don't remember him ever sitting in a chubby little heap like this one, clucking away happily and looking good enough to eat.'

'We're obviously much better babysitters than you ever were,' said Alice.

I turned to stare. Talk about soap opera episodes! My best friend Alice flirting with my mother's boyfriend!

What next? Whatever *next*?

'Woof!'

Next was my mum coming home. All of us heard her car pull up outside, the rattle of her key in the lock and the *thwack!* of her shaking the worst of the water off her raincoat before she hung it up. It was quite clear that Richard Naylor didn't want to startle her. 'Hi!' he called. 'Hi, Frances! We're in here. Four poor waifs sheltering from the storm.'

Mum appeared in the doorway. 'Here's a surprise!' she said. 'How are you, Alice? My, how Archie's grown! Is he actually *walking*?' Without waiting for an answer, she turned back towards the kitchen. 'More tea for anyone?'

'I'd love some,' Richard Naylor said. 'I'm soaked and frozen.' But he didn't do what we expected – that is, get up and follow her. He turned back to Archie on his hands and knees, pretending to be some sort of bear or dog. Archie looked rather unsure about the transformation. His lower lip stuck out the way it does before he starts to cry. But Richard Naylor had the sense to back away a bit and give him time.

'Woof!' he said gently. 'Woof!'

Alice was in there like a shot. 'Go on, Archie! Want

to pat the nice doggie?' She lifted his chubby little hand and bought it down a couple of times on Richard Naylor's head.

I rolled my eyes at her and, grinning, she took her hand away. Left to his own devices, Archie began to bash poor Richard Naylor on the head quite hard.

'Hey! Steady on!' he said. But it was in a sort of friendly dog voice, gruff but amiable. 'Don't thump the poor doggie's brains out.'

'Bev says that no one caring for a baby has a working brain anyhow,' Alice informed him. 'So you'll be fine.'

'Bev's Archie's mother,' I explained. 'We're giving her a break because Alice's mother reckons that if her sister's not careful, she will forget the person she was before.'

Now Mum was back in the doorway. She stood there with the mugs of tea she'd made, but came no closer. 'Bev might as well forget who she was before,' she told us in a crisp, almost irritable voice. 'Raising a child is like taking apart the life you've spent years building for yourself, and using all the bricks to make another life for someone else.'

I stared at her. I absolutely *stared*. The cheek of it! The *nerve*! Hadn't she just pulled my life apart without even asking me? Without a *thought*. And here she was, as good as whining about the hours that she'd had to spend on me even before she'd blown our family to pieces.

I wasn't the only one staring at her, either. So were

Richard and Alice. Quickly, she turned to leave the room, still holding both the mugs.

'So what was all that about?'

Looking a bit confused, Richard prised Archie's fingers out of his hair and scrambled to his feet. He left the room and shut the door behind him.

'So what was all that about?' whispered Alice.

I made a face. 'How should I know? She probably thinks we're in the way – ruining the nice quiet afternoon she'd planned to have alone with him.'

'She can't be annoyed with us for coming in out of that rainstorm,' Alice murmured. 'Nor with us having Archie. There must be more to it than that.' I watched her think it through. 'And what she said about children wasn't very nice.' Her eyes widened. 'Hey, Scarlet! You don't think that she was upset to see her boyfriend on the floor, mucking about with Archie?'

I didn't catch on straightaway. I just said sourly, 'If she's off kids herself, you'd think that she'd be glad that he's the one scrabbling about, being so nice to Archie.'

'Not if that makes it really clear he's good with kids, and likes spending time with them.'

I stared at Alice. 'You mean, *she* might not want them, but he will?'

Alice just shrugged, but I knew that was exactly what was in her mind.

And then a new thought struck. Richard had been perfectly happy on the floor, fooling about with Archie. He hadn't moved away the moment Mum came in. He hadn't stopped the game. He hadn't even looked the slightest bit uneasy.

He was a nice man, I knew that. And good at being tactful.

So it was crystal clear that my mum couldn't have told him yet what Dad told me – that she could not have any more babies at all.

The bricks of your own life

Later, I thought about how odd it was that I'd not shared with Alice what Dad had told me about Mum and babies. Alice and I talk about most things. Sometimes it takes a while before I feel like telling her everything that's on my mind. (I'm sure she's the same with me.) But I can't remember keeping proper secrets from her, and though the two of us never talk much about boys, or what marriage might be like, it was still strange of me not to pass on to her what Dad had told me.

We played with Archie till the rain had stopped, then took him home. For all that Mum had not looked thrilled to find us all sprawled on the floor with him, I noticed when I went to look for Archie's jacket, that she'd still thought to drape it over the radiator so it was warm and dry when we stuffed him back in it.

Back again at the new house, I sat on my cosy private window ledge and thought about all that – and what Mum said about using the bricks of your own life to build your child's. I suppose, simply from watching poor Bev, I'd learned that once you have a baby you can't fit in everything. I've seen her show up at her sister's house with horribly greasy hair and the sort of stains on her clothes that make people stare. Bev still had enough of a grip to notice and spoon out the reasons: 'I was about to have a shower when he started to squawk.' Or, 'I would have changed, but I knew if I didn't get him over here fast, I'd have to wait till he was fed again.' And I can understand that. Archie has sicked up on me more than once. But I can always borrow something clean from Alice, and take my stained blouse home – not like poor Bev, who's always pushed for time. 'I don't know where the hours go!' 'The days just get chewed up.'

But I didn't think that Mum had that sort of 'harried mum' thing in mind. I reckoned Alice was right, and she'd come home that afternoon with her own ideas about how her day would pan out. When she walked in to find the four of us all sprawled on the floor, she was fed up. Suddenly having to take me and Alice and Archie into account had really, really bugged her.

Would she have been bothered, back in the old house, when there was just the boring day-to-day stuff to get done? No, she'd been grumpy because Richard was about, and Alice and I were in the way, cramping her style. Hadn't she as good as announced to all of us that she'd been forced to throw away her no-doubt otherwise perfect life, in order to bring me up?

What sort of insult is *that*?

I wasn't going to let her get away with it. How was it our fault if it had started pelting with rain while we were so close to the house? Things like that happen. She should have thought about how much I might get in her way, even when I was older, before she went to all that trouble to have a baby at all! She should have thought ahead and realized you can't shove a daughter tidily away in a cupboard the moment you decide there's somebody more interesting in your life. The longer I thought about it, the more I reckoned that Mum was turning into another of those selfish parents in our class who've gone off to do their own thing, not bothering about anyone else in their family. Like Mia's mum, taking off for weeks on end on that pilgrimage to Santiago, then turning everything upside down with her new love affair. Or Greg's dad going to Dubai, and then just vanishing.

So she had taken a massive risk, giving me the scarlet book in hopes that she could poke her nose into my feelings. Why shouldn't she know exactly what I'd been thinking? No reason at all for me to feel guilty, or hold back for fear of hurting her. I *wanted* her to know exactly what I thought about everything she'd done, and how mean and self-centred she was being now. I knew, if she came up and found the book, she'd not even try to stop herself. She'd open the first page and start to check on me.

And wouldn't it serve her right to find that she was reading a heap of stuff about her own self!

Yes. Serve my mother right.

'Help!'

I picked up a pen. That's when I saw the message come in on my phone. It was from Alice. 'Help!'

I rang her back at once. 'What's up?'

'Disaster! It's Andy's birthday tomorrow and I forgot, so I've got nothing for him.'

'Tell him you owe him but he'll have to wait.'

'I can't do that! It's *Andy*!'

I knew exactly what she meant. Since that car accident, Andy's not been his happy-go-lucky old self at all. It's not just that he can't get about so easily. He takes things harder than he did before. Now that he can't burn up his energy like Alice and Ben, things like his birthday *matter*.

'OK,' I said. 'I'm getting my brain in gear here.'

But Alice had already worked it out. 'That book your mother gave you – the one that's all those shades of red . . .'

I looked down at it lying open in my lap. 'Yes?'

'That would get me out of this hole. I mean, it's really classy, but not girly. And if I'd decided to buy Andy a book with blank pages for his birthday, I could have chosen that one. He has been writing quite a lot – not just a sort of diary while he's getting better, but stories and poems as well. Even a few drawings. So I thought, since you said you hadn't started on it yet . . .'

Alice said that, and there it was, resting against my knees, still shiny and untouched. The perfect gift. But it was such bad timing! If she had asked me even ten minutes earlier, I would have said, 'No problem, Alice. Want to bike round and fetch it?'

But now I really didn't want to give it away. I had a plan for it, and for my plan to work, I needed either the scarlet book or one exactly the same. But I had no idea where Mum had bought it. If I gave Alice mine, what were the odds I'd find another?

Not good at all.

So I didn't give myself more time to think. I just said, 'Sorry, Alice. That's no good. I've already started on it.'

'Really?' said Alice. 'You can't have got very far. Can't we just tear those pages out?'

'It would look *terrible*.' I was still thinking fast. 'Look, I've an idea. Mum's just bought Dad a present for his birthday next week. It's lovely. It's a sort of bedside lamp that throws out silhouettes of old-fashioned men in frock coats and ladies in riding jackets cantering round and round.'

She couldn't have sounded more doubtful. 'Really, Scarlet? A bedside lamp with horsey silhouettes? That sounds a bit . . .'

She broke off. But I knew what she thought of my idea. Since Andy first came out of hospital unable to stand without wobbling, let alone walk, I've never once heard Alice use the word 'lame'.

No. Not for Andy, not for anyone.

I reckoned it was up to me to fill the sudden silence on the phone. And if the lamp had really been a rubbish present, I might have given up and offered her the scarlet book. ('Oh, look! The pages did tear out, and it looks fine.')

But I know Andy, and I know how many hours, even now, he's stuck in bed. I knew he'd like the lamp. I reckoned watching all the riders going round the room might even help him get to sleep at nights when bits of him are aching horribly.

It wasn't just from selfishness I talked it up. 'Honestly, Alice. Wait till you see it. It throws these amazing shadows round the room. It's mesmerizing. Mum and I put it on and switched out all the other lights, and it was magic.'

I could tell she was coming round to the idea. 'How much did your mum spend on it? I've only got three weeks' allowance.'

'I'm sure it wasn't more than that. But if it was, I'll help you out.'

'You *really* think it might be Andy's sort of thing?'

'Wait till you see it.'

'Can I come round and get it now?'

'No. I have to talk to Mum. I'll bring it in to school. And you can tell Andy tomorrow that you've a special reason for not handing over his present till the end of the day.'

'What would that be?'

'Simple. You want it to be *dark* so he can see what it does.'

There was another silence while she thought about it. 'Yes, that'll work,' she said at last. 'Thanks, Scarlet. You're a good mate.'

Not all that good, I thought. But I had no regrets. There was no way that I was giving up the scarlet book. No. Not for Andy, not for anyone.

That scarlet book was mine.

Had she gone looking?

I should have gone downstairs and asked Mum straightaway. I should have said, 'Emergency!' and told her Alice's problem. I'm ninety-nine per cent sure that she'd have rushed upstairs to fetch the lamp she'd bought for Dad's birthday and handed it over. 'You take it, Scarlet. I've time to buy another.'

But there was still that tiny one per cent of worry. I'd not earned any favours from Mum recently by being pleasant.

No choice, though. I had promised Alice. So I just waited till I knew that Mum was busy on the phone, then sneaked a chair onto the landing to lift the box down from the cupboard shelf where she had put it, out of the way.

I smuggled it up to my room, along with wrapping paper. First I took out the lamp and looked at it again. Perfect! Even just sitting on my desk and not switched on, it looked odd enough to attract anyone's attention. Tomorrow, when Mum was already halfway out of the house and in a hurry, I'd ask her casually where she had found it. ('Alice wants one for Andy.') Alice and I would buy another first thing on Saturday. It wasn't likely Mum would go to the cupboard to look at the present again before she took it down to wrap it for Dad's birthday, and that was a week away. But if she did, I would just say that I had taken it round to Alice's to show her, and I'd forgotten to bring it back.

The plan wasn't watertight, but it would probably work.

While I was cutting the wrapping paper to size, the box tipped over and a square of paper slid out. It was the sales receipt. At first I only looked to see how much the lamp had cost. (Cheaper than I'd have guessed.)

But then I noticed where Mum had bought it – Hatcher's Cross, and from the very same shop where Dad and I had bought the paint.

First, I was just annoyed. It was a pretty long way, and we were not allowed to ride our bikes along that road. We'd have to take the bus, and that would chew up most of Saturday morning.

But then I wondered why Mum had gone that far to look for something for Dad. If she's not shopping online, she usually gets presents of that sort from Niche Interiors, just half a mile away. To get this lamp, she must have driven through a million traffic lights, then found a parking space, then made her way to the far end of the mall.

It isn't like my mum to make more of a job than she needs out of anything. She's always said that's how she manages to keep the show on the road. (She means the house, her job and me.)

Had what I said about Laura made her dead curious? Had she gone looking for her? If I was going to spy on someone in a shop, I'd make sure that I had a brand-new carrier bag that had their logo on it to try to show I'd been in the place for some other purpose. I'd just pretend that – job done! – I was now simply strolling down the aisles to see what other things there were for sale. I could imagine Mum stopping to pick out a couple of those colour shade strips, pretending to inspect them while she kept her eyes peeled for some nice-looking shop lady coming her way to offer her some help.

She'd probably only let the woman get close so she could check her badge to see if it was Laura Deloy. Then she'd have turned away, muttering something along the lines of, 'No, really! I'm just fine. I have the samples I need. And I'm already late. But thanks!'

She'd have been off like a shot.

But it would still have been a chunk of time out of her day. Were people who split up usually so curious? Dad hadn't shown the slightest scrap of interest in Richard Naylor. He'd asked no questions about him at all.

Could Mum be jealous? Even regretting what she'd done? I know she had a boyfriend of her own, but maybe she'd assumed that Dad would simply settle down neatly and tidily to some boring life all alone. Maybe her finding out he had another woman in his sights had wobbled her a bit.

Well, good! I was so mad at her I didn't even want to think about what would be best for all of us. I was just glad she was rattled.

'And by the time I'm done,' I muttered to myself, 'you will be worse than rattled. Wait and see.'

'Any time, mate.'

Next morning I handed over the box I'd carried in to school so carefully. Alice shook off the starry blue paper I had folded round it.

'Did you bring sticky tape?'

'Of course.'

She eased the lamp out of its box and held it at arm's length in the corridor. 'It's weird. What are these silhouettes doing? Don't they block all the light?'

'You need to see it in the dark,' I told her. 'When it warms up, it spins. Those black and white bits make it look as if the horses and their riders are galloping round your bedroom walls.'

She still looked baffled.

'Come into the mop room,' I said. 'That's dark enough. I'll show you.'

'There are no plugs in the mop room.'

'OK, then. Dr Chohan's lab. She has those blackout blinds.'

I checked the time. We still had seven minutes before the bell. The lab was empty. Alice pressed buttons so the blinds came down while I plugged in the lamp, and fiddled with the shade till it was balanced.

We stood and watched. First slowly, then a little faster, round the walls of Dr Chohan's dark laboratory galloped the silhouettes of horses and riders. The riders sat straight-backed in their old-fashioned gear. The men had wide, showy moustaches and the women's hair was twisted into complicated buns. (No safety helmets back then.) The horses' legs did truly seem to move.

'You're right,' said Alice. 'It is *amazing*. I could watch this for hours.'

'Please don't,' I teased. 'Or we'll be very late for registration.'

She took to twirling on the spot, to follow one particular silhouette as it pranced around the room. 'How does it *work*?' she asked. 'It's not as if the horses' legs are actually moving. How come the riders look as if they're really cantering?'

All I did was shrug. But then a voice behind me – Dr Chohan's voice – broke in. 'For heaven's sake, Alice! It's simply a dissociation between the physical reality of what you're looking at, and your perception of it because of how your brain processes information.' She knocked off the science lecture to add, 'I do have to admit, it's rather fine.'

Alice unplugged the lamp. 'It's for my brother's birthday.' She lowered the lamp into the box and wrapped it properly. 'You are an angel, Scarlet. You've saved my life!'

'Any time, mate.'

She hugged the gift to her chest. 'He's going to love it. Just love it!'

I knew he would too. Ever since the accident, Andy has had to spend whole days in bed. Bits of him just go wrong. Sometimes he loses feeling in his legs. Sometimes his spine aches. Sometimes he even has seizures, and after those he often sleeps for hours and still feels groggy when he wakes. But there was something magical about the lamp. I could imagine him lying there, and the long hours passing far more easily as he watched his four riders canter around his room.

On our way out of school, I handed Alice another small wrapped gift. 'Here. Tell Andy that's from me.'

It was the only thing that I'd been able to find the night before. It was a magnifying glass that had a built-in light. I'd had it for a while, but I had polished up the lens and handle till you couldn't tell it from brand new.

To find it, I'd been forced to unpack all those last boxes I had been so stubbornly ignoring since our move to the new house.

But anything for Andy. Even that.

Mean stuff

That night, when Alice had been in touch ('He absolutely *loves* it!'), I thought a bit more about Andy. The trees outside were swaying towards my porthole window and casting creepy shadows across my wall. I suddenly found myself imagining her brother in his new, strangely high, hospital-style bed, and wondered if the gift had been a horrible mistake. How would someone who used to be so good at sports feel about watching those riders cantering so easily around his walls? Wouldn't it just rub things in? Till Andy's old enough to drive, and gets a special car, he won't be able to have that sort of free, speedy feeling. And even then, watching the fields flash past on either side can't be the same as striding over them, breathing sharp air in your lungs and knowing that your legs will take the strain without you even noticing that's what they're doing.

I felt so bad. I thought, if only I'd let Alice give him the scarlet book, he could have sat propped up in bed at nights and written in it everything he thought and felt. He would have had the perfect place to write about his problems, his frustrations, all his lost dreams. He needed it far more than

I did. I tried to console myself that Alice had said Andy was writing stories and poems, so it wouldn't have been the right present. Books like the one Mum gave me are good for keeping a diary and making resolutions, or copying things that are already perfect out in your neatest handwriting to keep for ever and ever. But if you started on a poem, all the corrections you made would spoil the look of it. And if it were a story, you'd do far better with a laptop.

I pulled out the scarlet book and ran my fingers over its perfect glossy cover. I was still glad I hadn't given it to Alice instead of the lamp. But I felt *awful*. How could it be that I could so determinedly tell lies to my best friend to keep hold of something so cool and beautiful, and yet the only thing that I could think to write in it was mean stuff to upset my mum?

Setbacks

Alice's brother was still on my mind by morning. Even before she'd locked up her bike, I'd brushed aside what she was telling me about her ride to school, and asked, 'How do you think it feels, being like Andy?'

Her face set and she turned away.

'You know,' I added quickly. 'Getting better so slowly and having to put up with setbacks.'

'There aren't so many setbacks,' Alice said firmly. 'All his consultants are really pleased with him.'

She says 'all his consultants' because he has more hospital appointments than I have suppers with Dad. There's one consultant for his legs, another for what's happened to his spine, and one who deals with all the drugs he has to take for seizures. He probably has more that I don't even know about.

I'm so dumb that even from the way that she was trying to keep ahead of me, striding towards the swing doors, I didn't realize just how much I was upsetting her. I simply tried to explain. 'I know he's getting better all the time,' I said. 'I can see that. I was just wondering if Andy ever feels really fed up with how long it's taking. Or if he ever worries about how much he'll be back to his old self when all his doctors finally say that they've done everything they can.'

She gave me such a fierce look that I was really glad to hear the bell. It gave us an excuse to separate.

'You're off to fetch your flute? I'll see you back in class.'

'How do you even *know* this?'

On my way down the corridor to our home room, Jake caught me. 'Scarlet, I need to talk to you.' He was already pulling me into the cleaning cupboard. 'In here, quick.'

'Ja-ake!' I complained. 'What are you doing?' But we were already inside. Leaving the door open a crack to let in light, he said, 'I have to tell you something, and it's important.'

For just a moment I was sure he was about to tell me my mum and Richard Naylor were getting married. But then I realized she was still married to my dad. It couldn't happen that fast.

Still, the idea had rattled me. It wasn't in the nicest tone of voice that I said, 'What's so important that you can't tell me in the corridor?'

'This is.' He took a breath. 'I think you can't know something I know about the accident.'

He'd baffled me. '*What* accident?'

'Andy's, of course. I was behind you in the bike shed when you were talking to Alice.'

I knew I'd put my foot in it from her response, so I told Jake defensively, 'All I asked Alice was—'

He interrupted me. 'I know! I heard. But what you don't know is that Alice thinks that awful crash was her fault.'

I stared at him, then said, 'But Alice wasn't even in the car. How could it possibly be her fault? How could she even *think* that?'

'Well, Alice does. At least, she did. A bit.'

'But *why*?'

There was a long and horrible pause. Then Jake said, 'I really shouldn't tell you this. I promised that I wouldn't.

But Alice told me that on the morning of the accident she'd tripped over one of Andy's football boots and been so irritated that she'd kicked it behind the coat rack, out of the way but also out of sight. So when he and Ben were getting ready to go off to footie practice that night, it took him a while to find it.'

'So?'

'So she thinks, if they'd crossed those lights even a minute earlier . . .'

'That's *crazy*! You can't look at accidents that way!'

'Sssh!' he said. 'Calm down, Scarlet. I know that. You know that. And Alice probably knows that too, most of the time. But back then—'

'Back *when*?' I was so furious. 'How do you even *know* this?'

'Because I found Alice crying her eyes out in this very cupboard.'

'And she told *you*?'

'I wormed it out of her, yes. But after she calmed down a bit, she made me promise that I'd never mention it again. Ever. Not to her, or to anyone.' He hesitated. 'But then, after I heard you—'

'That's OK, Jake,' I snapped. 'I get the picture! Thanks for telling me.'

I reached for the door handle, but he caught hold of my arm. 'What has got *into* you?' he demanded. 'I've told you something that I thought you needed to know, and maybe I shouldn't. But I still don't see why you're *angry*.'

I couldn't answer. I didn't even *know*. I wrenched my arm free. 'Lay off, Jake!'

He had the last word, though. 'Is it because she didn't tell you something and she told me instead? I'll bet it is! Well, let me tell you something, Scarlet. Only small kids think everything's to do with them. Maybe you should *grow up*.'

Her very best friend

I was so angry that I bunked off the first class. I was mad enough at Jake, but I didn't want to even *look* at Alice. How could she do that? How could she keep a secret as important as that from me, her very best friend?

But gradually, I calmed down. I knew she had her flute lesson, so as soon as the next bell rang I could sneak out of the cloakroom I was hiding in, back into class, and just be sitting in my normal place when she came in.

She'd clearly recovered from what I'd said in the bike shed because she just slid in beside me. 'Where *were* you? I looked *everywhere*.'

'Oh, I got snaffled,' I lied, 'to hold some weird bit of equipment steady for Dr Chohan while she fixed it.'

'Oh, good.' She patted my hand. 'I worried it might be because I was grumpy earlier. Sorry about that.'

'No need to apologize,' I told her. (And now I understood, of course, there clearly wasn't.)

'So we're still on for tomorrow?'

'Going to the mall to get another lamp? Yes, we're still on.'

'While we're here, Scarlet . . . ?'

We got the very last one.

'They went quite slowly till the day before yesterday,' the man in the shop said. 'Then someone came in and bought three.'

Alice gave me a nudge. 'That'll be Dr Chohan, needing them to invent an exam question on optical illusions.'

'It does *work*, doesn't it?' I asked the man. 'It's not just the last to go because it's a dud?'

'I'll plug it in and show you.'

'No,' I said, realizing it didn't matter. So long as it was in the cupboard when Mum went to wrap it, my problem had been solved. I think I must have been worrying about replacing it more than I let on, because I felt light-headed with relief, clutching the bag. So when Alice grinned and said, 'While we're here, Scarlet . . . ?'

I knew exactly what she had in mind. But still I made her say it. 'Yes? While we're here, Alice . . . ?'

'Shall we just take a peep along the paint aisle?'

I couldn't help grinning. 'You want to see the woman who made my dad blush to his hair roots?'

'Not *many* hair roots,' she teased. 'But yes. Why don't we creep along and take a peek at her.'

'We are not *creeping* anywhere,' I said. 'We have been buying things.' I lifted the bag. 'So I have every right to stroll along another aisle to show you the colour I would have chosen for the living room if I'd not been outvoted by Dad and Laura Deloy.'

We took our time – stopped at the brushes to take a casual look around. Backtracked to look at books of wall-paper samples. Picked out a few paint colours that Alice thought might look good in her own room 'if anyone ever gets around to it'.

No sign of Laura Deloy.

We had run out of ways to spend time in the empty aisle when finally I noticed the spiral stair at its far end, and thought to look up. Above us was an office. Behind its glass wall several women sat working on computers, and one stood watching us.

Laura.

Without even thinking, I waved.

She gave a quick wave back, and started for the spiral stair.

'Is that *her*?' Alice hissed. 'She's coming down! She's going to speak to us!'

'Why shouldn't she? She probably assumes we need some help choosing paint.'

'Oh, don't be such a dim bulb!' said Alice. 'She knows exactly who you are. She's coming down to ask after your dad.'

'Of course she isn't!'

'Want to bet?'

'Well,' I said irritably. 'It's too late to do a runner now. We'll have to stay and be polite.'

'What, tell her we were just gawping?'

'Sssh! Alice! Leave this to me!'

By now, Laura was almost beside us. 'Hi!' she said, smiling. 'Are you and your dad ready to start on another room?'

Dark purple. Maybe even black.

So she did know exactly who I was. 'Not yet,' I told her. Then, realizing that raised the question of why we had been lurking on her aisle, I pointed at Alice. 'My friend here is thinking of doing up her bedroom.'

'Really?' She looked at Alice. 'And have you any ideas about the kind of look you're after?'

145

Alice played along. 'I'd quite like to paint the whole room dark purple. Maybe even black.'

Laura Deloy smiled. 'I can't see your parents being very keen on either of those ideas.'

'No,' Alice conceded. 'They are non-starters, I suppose.'

'So. Any other colours?'

Before you knew it, the two of them were standing together poring over shade charts and chatting away like old mates. I felt quite left out. I wandered further along the aisle to look at the colours on the tiny tester pots. (I always want to buy some, but what I'd do with them, I've no idea.) Then I walked through the gap into bathroom fittings.

By the time I came back, Alice was clutching a sheaf of shade strips. 'Ready to go?'

'Ready.' I picked up the bag I'd left beside the two of them when I went wandering. Laura Deloy nodded at her shop's logo printed on the side. 'Successful trip?'

Without even thinking, I answered, 'Yes. It's a lamp. A present for Dad's birthday.'

'Is that very soon?'

I sussed at once that that was not a normal question. She'd never have asked that if she'd not taken far more interest in my dad than in the general run of customers. I wasn't going to answer, but Alice cheerfully barged in to fill the gap. 'Wednesday,' she said. 'This coming Wednesday.'

'Time to go,' I told Alice.

She grabbed my arm and almost waltzed us both along the aisle, waving thanks back at Laura as she went. 'That was a brilliant idea of yours,' she all but sang. 'I am so happy!'

'What?' I said. 'What was a brilliant idea of mine? Explain.'

'Painting my room. I didn't realize, till you came out with it, that that's exactly what I want to do.' She flipped her sheaf of paint card samples. 'Look at these! Oh, I'm so happy, Scarlet! Oh, I'm so happy!'

Pain

There was a price for Alice's new room, and not just the cost of paint. Mrs Henty told Alice that, in return for getting it all done up the way she wanted, she'd have to do more babysitting for Bev. The Hentys are the most amazing family for negotiating about anything – everything! – but no one in the house seems even to notice, let alone mind, how odd they are about that.

Mr Henty might start. 'Marcia,' he'll say to Alice's mum. 'Would you bring in those raspberry canes I left in the drive?'

'Sure,' Mrs Henty will say. 'If you'll take over peeling these potatoes.'

'I'll peel those potatoes if you put out the wheelie bins.'

'I'll put out the wheelie bins if you bring the vacuum cleaner down from Alice's room.'

'I'll bring down the vacuum cleaner if you find an envelope for Ben's football money.'

And on and on. Nobody ever seems to get ratty about it. And I'm not even sure they keep to all their deals. But Mrs Henty reckoned Bev was getting low in spirits and needed time to herself, and so she said if Alice wanted her room freshly decorated in the nice bright colour she chose, she'd have to put in a bit of time caring for Archie.

So we had Archie after school till suppertime two days in a row. The first was my last day at Mum's before Dad's birthday. Alice and Archie came there. We mucked about in my room for a while, then went downstairs to find a snack for Archie, who was getting grouchy.

Mum wasn't alone. Sometime while we'd been in my attic room, Richard Naylor had shown up. The two of them were on the sofa. (They weren't too close. I wondered if they'd shifted further apart while we were shepherding Archie down the stairs.)

Richard was in a cheery mood. 'Hi, Archie! Want to come and pull my hair as hard as you pull Alice's?'

Archie, of course, was far too young to understand a word of this peculiar greeting. Ignoring Richard entirely, he staggered over the rug and fell against an empty chair.

He grabbed at a cushion, but finding it no help in climbing up, turned and stretched out his arms.

I thought that he was looking at me. Certainly at me or Alice – we were side by side. But Richard Naylor was off that sofa in a flash to scoop him up. 'Coming to sit by me?'

'By me', you notice. Not 'by us'.

Mum moved a little to the side, to give him space. I watched her face. It was expressionless. If Dad hadn't told me that the chances of her having another child were zero, I'd have assumed her mind was somewhere else entirely – thinking ahead to some important meeting in the morning, or trying to remember what was in the fridge, and if she could offer everyone supper.

As it was, what I saw was pain.

I turned my head as if to watch Richard and Archie, squashed at their end of the sofa playing some stupid game with Richard's fingers. But I kept my eyes on Mum. Her face stayed set. She never once looked Richard and Archie's way. I saw her stretch her fingers on the sofa arm as if to start to drum in irritation, then snatch back her hand. I watched her shift about uncomfortably, then scramble to her feet.

'Anyone for tea?'

A nice big birthday surprise

'I'll have a cup,' said Richard, not even bothering to glance in Mum's direction. 'Thanks, Frances.'

'Me too,' said Alice, 'if you're making it. Can I have peppermint?'

Then I surprised myself. 'I'll come and help,' I told her.

Once we were in the kitchen, I tested out my theory that watching Richard Naylor getting on so well with a small child had made her miserable.

'He's very good with Archie,' I said as casually as I could.

'Oh yes,' she said. And though she tried to hide it, I'm sure I could hear bitterness in her voice. 'He is a man who really, *really* ought to have children.'

It made me wonder why she'd taken up with him before she'd had this sorted out. Mum's always taken an interest in what we do in Personal Development classes. ('We really could have done with those back when I was in school!') And only the term before, when Mrs Bennet was teaching a session on Dating, I'd told Mum she'd been going on about the fact that couples should check that they're compatible about the basics. And whether you plan to have a family or not was one of her very first examples.

Can you be too in love to even *think*?

After the tea, Richard gave Alice and Archie a lift home, and Mum looked horribly flat. I felt so sorry for her that, on an impulse, I asked, 'Will you be coming over to Dad's tomorrow?'

She sounded startled. 'What, for his birthday?' I watched the idea sink in. 'Why not? I have a present for him, after all. I could drop by and stay for a quick drink.'

'I think he'd really like that.'

She smiled. 'I think that I would too.'

It suddenly looked so *simple*. If things with Richard were far more complicated than she'd first thought, then Dad would seem a better bet than he had done before. Mum might even look at him and think: You're not too bad. And we got on for years. We could try again. And he might think: I really miss you, Frances. And I'm not sure I want to start again with someone new. So let's just have another go, and I will try to be a little more exciting.

It might work out.

Worth a try, anyhow. 'So shall I tell him you're coming?' I said. 'Or would you rather be a surprise?'

She reached an arm round my waist, and gave me a squeeze. 'What do you think?'

'I think you ought to be a nice big birthday surprise,' I told her.

'I'm not *that* big,' she teased. But she was clearly pleased. She slid an arm round me, and I turned to put my arms round her and give her even more of a hug than she'd just given me. It seemed to me that we'd been treading on eggshells around one another ever since we moved out of the old house and into the places Richard owned.

So being close to her again felt good.

'Have you come home to nag?'

Next day at school, as I was gathering up my stuff to go home, Jake pounced. 'Am I forgiven?'

I kept my end up. 'What for? What have you done?'

'You know. For saying what I did.'

I certainly didn't want him to repeat it. Quickly I said, 'Oh, that! I had forgotten about that.'

He clearly didn't believe me, but didn't push it. Instead, he offered me a finger of his chocolate bar and said, 'So I've moved back from zero to hero?'

I let out a scornful groan, but I like Jake, so took the chocolate.

I was still feeling good when I reached Dad's house. I found him standing on a chair in the kitchen, merrily humming *Happy Birthday* to himself. 'A-ha!' I said. 'Hanging yourself because you're now too old to want to keep on living? Or fixing up balloons?'

'Oh, very funny, Scarlet.' He twisted out the light bulb that had blown and reached in his pocket for the replacement. Before he'd screwed it even halfway in, on came the light.

'That's very naughty,' I told him. 'You always told me you should only fiddle with light sockets when you're sure the current is switched off.'

'When there's a switch at both ends of a room, it's hard to work out if the light's supposed to be on or off.'

'You told me, if I wasn't sure, I was to turn that circuit off at the fuse box.'

'Have you come home to celebrate my birthday, or to nag?'

'Whatever it takes.' I pulled the gift I'd found for him out of my school bag. 'Happy birthday, Dad!'

He stripped off the wrapping paper as roughly as a child of three. (Mum does it carefully, hoping to use it again.) My present was a radio-controlled mouse. I'd seen them outside the hardware store. The woman selling them was skilled enough at the controls to make the mouse look so real it would startle anyone.

Dad slid the batteries in and had a go. The mouse was pretty jerky at the start, but Dad is good at things like this and he soon had it skittering around the kitchen floor in a creepily convincing way.

'Let's see if it works on the carpet.'

He started to walk through, but I had seen a Penny's Place box on the side. 'Have you got strawberry tarts in there?'

'I have indeed.'

'Your birthday, but my treat?'

'I rather hoped that you might let me have one.' Already his attention was back on the mouse. I put the kettle on, and raised the lid of the box. 'Six!'

'Special offer.'

I made the tea while he kept playing with the mouse controls and muttering to himself. 'Bit of a left-hand lean there . . . Ah, not so keen on slopes . . . Oh, excellent! Who would have thought it could do a turn as sharp as that without tipping over?'

'There!' I said. 'Now you'll have something to play with every time your main assembly line packs up.'

'I'm not taking this into work! No one would get any-thing done.' He looked up for the first time since he'd slid in the batteries. 'This is the most wonderful thing, Scarlet. Where on earth did you find it?'

'At Hatcher's Cross.'

'Ah, Hatcher's Cross,' he said, and blushed. Turning his head away, towards the front window, he ploughed on, 'Speaking of Hatcher's Cross, Scarlet, there's something I've been meaning . . .'

Then he broke off. We could both see her out there. Laura

Deloy. She was trying to open the gate, and it was taking her a bit of time to lift the latch because she was carrying a shiny silver cardboard box with lots of fancy bright ribbons. I was appalled. All I could think was that Mum might arrive any minute and she would think that I'd persuaded her to come out of pure spite.

I turned on Dad. 'You should have *told* me you'd invited Laura!'

Dad looked bemused. 'I didn't. I had no idea that she was coming.'

I hissed, 'Well, how else does she know that it's your *birthday*?' And then I realized. Of course. Alice had told her.

'I'll have to let her in.'

Already Dad was on his way to the door. 'I'll have to let her in. She will have seen us.'

I wondered whether to run upstairs and hide till Laura had gone. *If* she was going to go . . . For all I knew, she and my dad were already locked in some great passionate affair. Perhaps the present in the box was a skimpy silk nightie – or worse! But somehow I stayed rooted to the spot while he said something cheerful and welcoming to Laura, and she stepped in the hall and walked in front of him into the room.

'Scarlet!' she said. 'Oh, I'm delighted you're here.'

I'm not an idiot. I saw the tiny 'so-have-you-told-her?' look that she gave Dad, and the small shake of the head that Dad gave back.

Again, Laura turned to me. 'I hope I'm not too much of a surprise. And if you two have plans, don't for a moment worry that I'm staying long enough to spoil them. I only wanted to come by to drop this off.'

She thrust the box at Dad who, true to form, tugged at the bows and ribbons without even stopping to admire them. He lifted the lid. 'A birthday cake!' He raised his head to stare at her. 'But how on earth did you know?'

'Oh, a little bird told me.'

If she looks my way, I thought, I am going to *scream*. But there was nothing coy and flirty about the way she said it. She was just brushing the whole business aside.

Dad isn't the persistent sort. Maybe he just assumed that she'd caught sight of some bit of official paperwork lying around when she'd come to admire the room. In any event, he didn't press her, only said, 'Well, since you're here, stay for tea.' He looked in my direction. 'Scarlet?'

'I'll get another mug.'

While I was in the kitchen, I heard him thanking her properly for the cake. I didn't know whether or not to carry in the strawberry tarts. Perhaps it would seem rude not to choose the cake on what was, after all, the perfect day for it. (At least she wouldn't have brought candles with her. Not forty-three of them. We wouldn't have to *sing*.)

But in the end I reckoned, if she'd come round as a surprise, she'd have to take her chances. The cake she'd brought with her might look amazing – and it did. But it might not be one of the kinds I like. And anyway I wanted strawberry tarts. So I brought in the plates and a big knife, and then the tarts from Penny's Place, and set the whole lot down on the coffee table. Then I sat on the sofa and waited for her to give me a friendly 'Dad's-new-girlfriend' smile, and start off with what I assumed would be the usual run of adult questions, starting with, 'So how's school, Scarlet?'

It never happened. Laura just pitched in. 'Your good friend Alice! Her face has been haunting me ever since Saturday. I'm *sure* I know her. I'm just sure I do.'

'Her name's not *Henty*, is it?'

I glanced at Dad. I wasn't keen on Laura letting on that my best friend and I had spent time nosing up and down her paint aisle simply so Alice could take a peek at his new girlfriend. I'd hoped that Laura Deloy would just exchange a few quick words while eating up the slice of cake I'd handed her, drink up her tea as fast as possible, and then push off – hopefully before Mum arrived.

I tried to float the idea that we'd all happened to bump into one another somewhere. 'I expect you've seen her before, out and about in town.'

'No, I don't think so.'

'Our school's pretty central, and she has to cycle quite a way to get there.'

But Laura Deloy wasn't buying it. 'Her face is so *familiar*. She's not a twin, by any chance?'

'No. She has brothers. But Andy's older and Ben's only eight.'

'Andy . . .' I watched the penny drop. She put her plate back on the coffee table. 'Her name's not *Henty*, is it?'

'Yes. Alice Henty.'

Laura's face cleared. 'Well, that explains it! I got to know her brother while he was in the spinal unit.'

'Really?'

Dad was surprised too. 'So were you working at the hospital back then?'

Laura Deloy shook her head. 'No. I was in the shop, but in soft furnishings, and Andy's mum kept coming in every few days, buying all sorts of pillows and cushions and bolsters, then bringing most of them back. So in the end I asked her what the problem was, and she explained. I showed her all our blocks of foam and sponge materials, and how they could be cut to shape.' She put on one of those looks that people use to show they're being super-modest. 'I suppose I somehow found myself offering to come and help with the measuring.'

If I'd been sitting next to Alice, I would have whispered, 'Busybody!' and hoped even harder that she'd go. Even Dad said, 'But surely the hospital does that? They're the ones with experience.'

Laura Deloy shrugged. 'They did explain exactly what he needed. But getting it done for the Hentys was far, far quicker than waiting for the hospital professionals to get it organized.' She took a ladylike nibble of cake. 'And Marcia was so keen to get Andy home.'

So she called Mrs Henty 'Marcia'. Suspiciously I asked, 'Then how come you never met Alice?'

'She and the younger brother were pretty well farmed out with other families through the worst of it.'

'Farmed out!' I grinned at Dad. 'You never realized we were running a farm back then, did you?'

He chuckled. 'Mooo!'

'Oink, oink.'

'Cluck, cluck.'

That's when she cottoned on. 'So Alice stayed with *you*?' and burst out laughing.

So it was just my rotten lousy luck that that's how Mum found us – sitting in front of the most splendiferous cake, mugs in our hands and laughing.

'Ouch!'

You wouldn't think the temperature could drop so fast. 'I am so sorry,' Mum said frostily. 'I don't think you can have heard me knocking, and I made the big mistake of letting myself in.'

She wouldn't even *look* at me. She nodded coolly at Laura, and came in the room only far enough to dump Dad's present on the nearest chair. 'I'll leave this here.'

'Stay for a cup of tea and slice of cake,' begged Dad. 'And let me introduce—'

But Mum was having none of it. 'No, really, Tony. I'm in a massive rush. I have to get back to the hospital. It's an emergency.' She was already halfway out of the door. 'I only came to wish you a very happy birthday. But I can see that you're already having that!'

And she was gone.

Laura Deloy made a face. 'Ouch!'

I could have *killed* her. I didn't know who I was madder at – Laura Deloy for muscling her way into our house in the first place, or Mum for instantly assuming that I'd played such a spiteful trick.

Dad said, 'Fran isn't like that normally. You must believe me. She really isn't like that.'

'That's right,' I said. 'Her coming round right now was just a stupid accident.'

Dad asked, 'How so?' And I could see it really mattered to him.

'Mum had your present ready,' I explained. 'I suppose she thought I'd bring it round with mine. But I persuaded her to come for tea, and it was me who thought it would be nice if she surprised you.' I turned to Laura. 'I didn't know that *you'd* be here!'

I can't say that I said it all that pleasantly. But, even so, I could tell that Dad was glad to hear it. 'Yes, then,' he said. 'Scarlet's right. It was an *accident*.'

The way he said it irritated me. It was the way he would have said it back when I was *three* and fretting that I'd broken a dish or a lamp. Then he went on to treat me as if I were even more of a baby. 'Scarlet, it's not your fault at all. I know you meant well. If Laura hadn't sussed out that it was my birthday, it would have been just you and me . . .'

He didn't add, '. . . and rather flat and lonely', but it was perfectly clear that's what he meant.

I scowled. But all that did was encourage Laura Deloy to poke her nose in. 'It's my fault too. I really should have thought. It was a silly thing, to come here uninvited on your actual birthday.'

Dad wasn't having that. 'No. Not at all. It's just a chapter of small accidents, and it'll be all right.'

'For *you*,' I told Dad bitterly. 'But not for *me*. Mum won't believe I didn't set her up on purpose. You could tell she was livid.'

He made a rueful Into-the-Valley-of-Death sort of face. 'I'll take you back round there as soon as we've finished our tea and I'll explain the whole thing to your mum.'

I was still furious. 'She won't believe you. She'll just think that you're sticking up for me.'

'I'll *make* her believe me.'

'Good luck with that,' I said sarcastically. But I did feel a little better. It must have been quite clear to both of them that I couldn't wait to get the mix-up sorted. So Laura Deloy pushed away the last of her bite of cake and rose to her feet. 'I must be off in any case.'

I heard Dad saying softly as she left, 'When will I see you again?'

She wasn't going to whisper. 'I'll give you a ring,' she told him in a tone of voice that seemed to mean, 'As soon as I am up for another giant dose of embarrassment.'

Mad as I was at her, I couldn't blame her for that. Anyone in her position would have assumed my dad still needed unravelling from my mum.

If I'd been her, I would have run a mile.

Suing for peace

As soon as we reached the house, I shoved my key into the lock. Dad's hand slid over mine. 'Ringing the bell might be wiser.'

'I *live* here,' I said irritably.

'Yes, but I don't. And your mum might not be alone.'

I hadn't thought of that. I rang the bell, and waited. A door inside slammed almost straightaway, but it seemed ages before Mum opened the door. 'Hello?'

From her frostbitten tone, it was quite clear to both of us what that hello actually meant, so Dad did answer her as if she had truly snarled, 'What do *you* want?'

'We've come to sue for peace.'

'I wasn't aware that we'd been quarrelling.' Her tone was still icy, and she was on the verge of slamming the door, but stopped herself in time.

'Listen,' Dad said. 'All that back there. It was a stupid accident. I didn't know that Laura Deloy was coming round. Neither did Scarlet. But Laura had somehow worked out that it was my birthday and showed up totally out of the blue with that cake. So Scarlet is *blameless*. You can't be mad at her. It isn't fair.'

Good old Dad.

Mum softened up enough to say, 'Odd that this Laura of yours knew that it was your birthday . . .'

I wasn't going to muddy the water by explaining that was Alice's fault. I just kept quiet, waiting for Dad to snap back at Mum's remark with, 'She's not *my* Laura.'

But he just shrugged. 'Look, Fran,' he said, 'we have come round to make sure you understand that there was no plan to make the two of you bump into one another. Scarlet had no intention of embarrassing you. Or embarrassing *any* of us. She asked you to come round in all good faith because she thought it would be nice for me, and you would make a lovely surprise.'

I could tell from her face that this time she believed him. 'I'm sorry. I misunderstood.'

Dad tried to help out. 'And I can see why you thought what you did.'

Mum said uncomfortably, 'I hope you'll make it clear to Laura that it was not her being there that so upset me. It was the thought that my daughter might be deliberately being spiteful and mean.' She turned to me. 'I'm sorry, Scarlet. It was an awful thing to think about you.'

If I'd been her, I'd probably have thought the same. But I wasn't going to let her off the hook that easily. So all I said was, 'That's OK.'

She held out her arms to me. 'Friends again?'

What could I say, with Dad there watching me? 'All right, then. Friends.'

We shared a hug.

'Now we'll be off,' said Dad.

Mum threw the door wide open. 'Oh, come on, Tony. It's still your birthday. Come in and have a drink.'

'No,' Dad said. 'We'll get back. We really did come round only to get this sorted.'

'I'm very glad you did. Thank you.'

Waving, she shut the door and we walked back to the car. Me, I was thinking hard. This was an evening when Mum knew I would be away. But she'd invited Dad in for a drink. She couldn't have been sure how long he'd stay. And after what just happened at his house, she certainly wouldn't have risked an action replay in reverse: her boyfriend showing up, surprising him.

So Richard Naylor wasn't coming round.

Again.

Oh, thanks, Alice! Thanks a bunch!

I couldn't wait to phone Alice and describe the afternoon in all its gory detail. And, 'Guess what! It turns out Laura knows your mum.'

'Knows her? But how? Nothing in our house has been painted for a hundred years.'

When I explained, Alice was quiet for a moment. Then she said, 'That means that Andy must have met Laura too – if she was in the hospital to measure stuff to fit him.'

'Ask him.'

'We'll ask them both. Should we let on your dad and Laura are getting to be pretty close, and she might end up as your stepmother?'

Oh, thanks, Alice! Thanks a bunch! It isn't that I hadn't thought of it. But hearing my best friend coming out with it so bluntly was still a shock.

She didn't notice that I hadn't answered her. She was still busy plotting. 'No. Best to say nothing about that. That way, they won't feel that they need to be polite, and we'll hear what they really think of her. I know! Come back with me after school. I'll ask if you can stay for supper.'

'I'm still at Dad's tomorrow.'

Alice brushed this aside. 'You're spending all tonight with him, so he won't mind.'

'I suppose not. Not if I don't stay late.'

So that was settled. Dad and I had a quiet evening. I did a bit of homework and we watched a film. As it was his birthday, he got to choose one of his ancient favourites: *Airplane!* (I won't admit it to him, but I love it too.) Then he had a bath, I had a shower, and we were ready for bed.

'Goodnight,' he said. 'I know I won't see you in the morning. Make sure you have a sensible breakfast and leave for school in good time.'

'Can I stop off at Alice's before coming home?'

Dad shrugged. 'You won't be late?'

'No. It's Ben's footie night, so Mrs Henty will drop me back here on the way.'

'That's fine by me.'

I didn't mention eating supper there. I reckoned if I had to make a stab at eating twice it was unlikely to kill me.

An angel sent from heaven

The Hentys' meal kicked off as usual, with Mr and Mrs Henty arguing ferociously about the new district housing plan. Alice's dad thought the more houses that were built, the better. Her mum insisted that would mean that either most of the green places round the town would be ruined, or contractors would be building on flood plains. 'And that's a dreadful thing to do. There's nothing more miserable than a flooded house.'

They batted on at one another till Alice managed to interrupt. 'I have a question. It's about Laura Deloy.'

'Laura Deloy?' Mrs Henty's face crumpled in thought. 'Oh, you mean *Laura*.'

'Yes,' Alice said patiently. 'Laura Deloy. She says she knows you and Andy from the hospital.'

'Indeed she does,' said Mrs Henty. 'But where on earth did *you* meet her?'

'In the paint aisle at the mall.' Alice pointed her fork at me across the table. 'When Scarlet and I were looking at colours for my room.'

'Don't use your fork as a pointer,' Mr Henty scolded.

'This Laura doesn't know *me*,' said Andy. 'I've never heard of her.'

'You wouldn't know if you had met the Queen while you were in that hospital,' said Mrs Henty. 'You were away with the fairies. They'd pumped so many drugs in you that you barely recognized me or your father.'

'You called me "Willow Parker" twice,' said Mr Henty.

I said to Andy, 'How come you even *know* Willow Parker? She's in our year group, not yours.'

'I don't,' said Andy. 'The fairies I was away with must have introduced us to one another while I was off my head.'

Alice turned back to her mum. 'So did you *like* her?' she persisted.

'Who?' Ben interrupted, baffled. 'This Willow Parker or this Laura Deloy?'

'Laura Deloy.'

I was amazed by Mrs Henty's response. '*Like* her? She was an angel sent from heaven! She was *amazing*. Nobody could have put themselves out more. She even came to the hospital after work to take a look at Andy, and give advice on which sort of foam block to get and how to cut it to size. She was the one who dared pin down the consultant in the corridor – actually stopped the woman in her tracks – to make her come to check that we were doing things the way they should be done. And it was Laura who told us who'd be best at making a cover for the foam block, and which material to choose for that. She was just *wonderful*.'

'If she was such an angel,' Alice said, 'how come I never met her before Scarlet and I bumped into her in the paint aisle? How come she's never been round here? Why wasn't she at that big party we had when Andy finally got onto crutches?'

'I'm sure she was invited. Yes, she was!' Now it was Mrs Henty's turn to point her fork across the table, but Mr Henty didn't say a word. 'I even remember exactly why Laura couldn't make it. She has twin sons and one of them was getting married that weekend.' She speared an olive off her plate and added casually, 'I've only ever met the other one. He was in the hospital car park, waiting to pick up his mum and run her to some garage that had fixed her car. He's not a bit like her. She's quite light-skinned and he's much darker. Laura says the father's family came from the Caribbean.' She pushed her chair back. 'Oh, and he has the most piercing whistle you've ever heard. Truly. Like a

169

drill through the head.' She turned to Ben. 'Finished? Then get your gear together quickly or you'll be late again. Scarlet, we're dropping you off, aren't we? Got all your school stuff? Are you ready to go?'

I wasn't sorry to get out of there. I'd caught the wink Alice had sent across the table and knew what was in her mind. My best friend thought, the way that things were going in my family I was set fair to get not just a handsome stepfather on one side who'd improve my Maths, but on the other two grown stepbrothers, and a stepmother who'd enrich my life with birthday cakes in lavishly beribboned boxes.

Awash

I know that if the scarlet book had been at Dad's house that night, I would have opened it and poured my heart out. And not to bitch at Mum. I would have covered pages with stuff to do with *me*. I was *awash* with feelings. Everything seemed to be spinning out of control. It was all right for Alice to think the changes round me were interesting, and even funny. Maybe they were. But it was my *life*. And I had no idea which of the things that swirled around in my head were going to happen, and which weren't.

No thanks to *them*. Oh, they're quite happy to turn your

life upside down to suit themselves, but they don't bother to tell you anything. Not *anything*. Take when Dad drove us back to explain the mix-up. I thought it was really odd that Mum invited Dad in. His birthday was the only evening she could have placed a bet well in advance that I'd stay at Dad's place. She would have had no reason on earth to think we'd end up on her doorstep. If she and Richard Naylor were so involved that she'd left Dad for him, and he had pretty well given her a house, wouldn't you think they would spend as much time together as they could? Had it been simple bad luck? Did he just happen to be working out of town?

Or had they fallen out?

I counted back the days since Richard Naylor had been sprawling on the floor, letting Archie grasp chunks of his hair. Had Mum seen him since? Now I thought back, she hadn't mentioned him to me. Not once. Had he been dumped? Or dumped her? Was that why it had been so easy to persuade her to come round to Dad's? And had that been another reason (over and above her thinking I'd been mean) why she'd been so upset to find Laura Deloy sitting with Dad on the sofa, having a good time?

How would I ever know, if no one ever bothered to tell me anything?

As for Dad, I'd no idea what might be going on there. Were he and Laura getting it together? Was Alice right? Would I end up with a stepmother and two grown stepbrothers? I'd like to have believed that Laura was just a busybody – some meddling do-gooder who would begin to irritate him if she kept showing up knee-deep in cakes and paint charts. But that's not how it looked. Wasn't Dad on the verge of telling me something about her when she arrived? And I had definitely not imagined that quick 'so-have-you-told-her?' look she shot him when she came in.

On the other hand, she'd gone to far more trouble than she needed with the Hentys, and she'd not fallen in love with anybody in that family. She'd simply put herself out for them in the kindest fashion – happy to spend time helping them out. They certainly didn't think of her as a nosy meddler.

So maybe this Laura was just one of those people who make friends easily and are generous with time and effort, and Dad had nothing real to blush about. Laura had seemed so relaxed. So easy. Maybe she'd simply told him that she'd be happy to go with him to the occasional film, or out for supper. Perhaps she was the sort who always felt compelled to offer people what she thought they needed. Mum used to tell me about a girl she'd grown up with at school. Someone called Maisie. 'She *had* to be helpful,' Mum said. 'Not just sometimes, but all day, every day. It must have been a pathology! She was forever rushing to set out the mats for gym, or jumping up from her seat to collect everyone's worksheets. Before the teachers even gave a thought to what needed doing next, Maisie had already done it. Her name was Maisie Grove, but she was so *irritating* that, behind her back, we called her Maisie Grovel.'

Perhaps this Laura Deloy was weird in the same way. Perhaps the only thing she had in mind was that Dad needed help in choosing paint, and it might be nice if someone dropped by to admire his handiwork. Then, knowing that his wife had left him recently, she might have thought it was a good idea to bring a cake on what she imagined might be a dismal birthday. Maybe Dad misunderstood, and if he hinted that he wanted to be more than a friend, she would be horrified. 'Oh, Tony! No, I'm sorry, but you've read me completely wrong!'

But maybe that idea had never crossed Dad's mind, and all he was about to tell me when she showed up was that the two of them might go together to a film one night. Dad hadn't dated anyone for nearly twenty years, so that idea alone might make him blush.

Maybe . . . Maybe . . . How would I ever know? They had been acting for weeks as if what I thought didn't matter in the slightest: Oh, don't bother telling Scarlet what's going on! What's it to *her*?

I was awash with feelings and completely at sea.

'Ooh, la la!'

Next morning it was my turn to go looking for Jake. He wasn't hard to find. Before I'd even crossed the courtyard I caught sight of him in the staff car park, watching The Menu write *Broccoli is deadly poisonous – a well-known fact* in the grime on the back of Mrs Tanner's car.

'Busy?' I asked.

'Just killing time till the bell rings.'

'Why? Is one of your many admirers lying in wait for you in the building?'

He grinned. 'You're such a smart one, Scarlet.' Turning his back on Mrs Tanner's car, he added amiably, 'How's tricks?'

'I cruise along,' I told him. 'And how are you and your handsome uncle Richard these days?'

It was a sort of trap. I'd thought it out. I reckoned that if his family knew that things between my mother and his uncle had collapsed, I would be able to tell from his response. He'd look more serious, and say, 'Fine, I guess. How's your mum taking it?' But if he thought the two of them were still ticking along happily, he'd be more likely to say something like, 'You probably know the answer to that better than I do.'

In fact all he did was shrug, then grab my arm, hissing, 'Quick, Scarlet! Duck!'

He held my arm so tight I had no choice. Once we were safely below the level of the car window, he put a finger to his lips and signalled me to follow him, keeping bent over, till we were several more cars down the row.

'Mrs Tanner?'

'She must have come back for something. She would have thought we wrote that stuff about broccoli.'

We heard the click of her car door opening and, moments later, a hefty clunk as it slammed shut.

We gave it a little longer, then stood upright. On one side Mrs Tanner was disappearing through the swing doors into school, but on the other Bicky was standing a short way away, making a stupid face. 'Ooh, la la! Jake and Scarlet! I've caught you at it.'

'You have indeed!' said Jake. He turned to me. 'Scarlet, my angel. We are discovered! Our secret love will soon be known to all!'

Jake is in drama club. I'm not. But I still made a pretty good performance of raising the back of a limp hand to my brow and whimpering, 'Oh, Jacob! Shall I be driven out of school in sore disgrace?'

I could tell Bicky wasn't too taken with my act. She was busy staring at Jake. 'Is that your real name? *Jacob?*'

'Nothing odd about that,' Jake said. He kept his face

dead straight. 'After all, everyone knows that anyone called Bicky must have the real name Biscuit.'

We left her trailing after us, wailing, 'My name's Rebecca! Bicky's just how my baby sister used to say it.'

'Was she the stalker you were trying to avoid?' I asked Jake as we reached our home-room door.

He nodded just as Mrs Tanner stormed past on her way back to the car park, brandishing a cloth. Then he took off for his locker.

I wondered what it must be like to have someone you don't even care about getting in your face whenever they can. I know that it would drive me mad. If someone kept prancing around me, making their eyes go big in that annoying way, they'd find themselves pretty sharpish in the nearest puddle.

But though she acts in such an idiotic way, Bicky is pretty. Maybe Jake was getting a little bit soppy about her.

I really hoped he wasn't. That would have sent him straight back down my personal estimation chute again – from hero to zero.

Zilch

I watched Mum like a hawk over the days that I was back with her. There were a couple of calls that might have been from Richard. She seemed to get a lot of texts. But he never once came to the house. Each afternoon I wandered in from school and made myself a snack. I'd spread my books over the kitchen table and start on homework. Then we'd have supper. After that, I'd go upstairs and get in touch with Alice. Then, if it wasn't too late, I might phone Dad before I went to bed.

Each day I thought, She'll have to crack. She'll have to ask me about Laura, then I can ask about Richard.

But nothing doing. Not a word. Not even a sideways hint along the lines of, 'I'm glad your dad won't be so lonely any more,' or, 'I wonder if this Laura has ideas for decorating more rooms in that house.'

Zilch.

On the last day I told her I'd be back with Dad over the weekend. Go for it, Mum! I urged her inwardly. Ask something casual like, 'Do you suppose that you might get to see Laura?'

Nothing again. I was the one who cracked. 'Where's Richard gone?'

'Sorry?'

Oh, please! Perfectly simple question. 'Where's Richard gone? I haven't seen him in ages. Is he away? Or ill?'

There was a long, long silence. I was surprised by that. Surely it must have struck her that I was going to ask about him sometime. You'd think she'd have her answer well thought out. I know if I had given some boy the final flick, or been blown off myself, I'd have been practising what I was going to tell my family until I was word perfect.

But all she said was, 'Richard and I are spending a little time apart. He's busy with something.'

'What sort of something?'

I watched her trying to damp down irritation at my persistence. 'If you must know, he's taking time to think.'

'About what? Whether or not he wants a life without children of his very own?'

She absolutely *stared*. 'How do you know?'

'Remarkable.'

Oh, really! Did she think I was intergalactically stupid? 'I saw him on the floor with Archie.'

Mum shook her head in wonder. 'Scarlet, you are *remarkable*.'

'It wasn't that hard to work out,' I said. 'You don't sit through all Mrs Bennet's Personal Development classes without learning that's the sort of thing new couples are supposed to think about.'

'Still . . .'

I didn't want to annoy her. But my next question burst out straightaway. 'Hadn't you talked about it *before*?'

'Before?'

'Before you left Dad and we moved in here.'

She got quite testy at that. 'Scarlet, I would have left your father in any case. Our marriage was as good as over.'

I'm not that easily derailed. 'Well, then,' I said, 'before you and Richard got so chummy.'

'I think that maybe Richard didn't properly realize . . .'

She broke off, so I finished the sentence for her. '. . . till he saw Archie?'

She shook her head as if she didn't want to think about it. 'Maybe. Yes, I suppose so. Probably.'

I picked my way as carefully as I could. 'But you're not *old*,' I said. 'And even if there are *problems*, these days there are other ways to have a baby.'

'Oh, Scarlet! I know that. But I see so many of these women in the hospital. I know the drawbacks all too well – and the poor odds.'

I don't know why I kept pushing her. It's not as if she wouldn't already have thought the whole business through for herself. 'Well, what about those people who have the baby for you?'

'Surrogate mums?' She turned away. 'No, I don't think so, Scarlet.'

'Adoption? Though I suppose . . .'

I didn't finish the sentence I had in mind. I had been thinking more about Richard's possible response to that idea than about hers. After all, he and Mum had only got together recently. And he would know that he could still have children of his very own with someone else.

In any case, I'd gone too far. Mum was moving towards the door. And I could understand why. I'd not forgotten what Dad said about what it meant to them. *Tears ran too deep.*

But who wants to stand in a kitchen anyway, comforting their mum because she's having problems with a boyfriend? Not me. I mumbled something about having to sort the Maths homework out by myself if Richard wasn't coming, then ran upstairs. But once I was up there, safe on my own, I couldn't think why I was feeling so different from when I'd sat in my room at Dad's, wishing so hard I'd had the scarlet book there, so I could write in it to sort out my feelings. Now here I was, just three days later, pretty well calm and settled.

Yes, things were sad for Mum. And I could almost think they might be sad for me. I'd never in a million years have told this to my mum, but ever since Bev had Archie, I've had a soft spot for babies. I know he's special, and masses of the babies you see about look far more trouble than they're worth. Still, knowing Archie had made me come round secretly to the idea that having a baby half-brother or sister might be nice. After all, Motty manages. And Helena's little brother is only two. So I could almost imagine feeling sorry about never having that. Oh, I knew things might change. After all, Richard Naylor might decide he didn't care at all about having a baby of his very own. He might just hurry back.

Or he might never be seen again.

But either way, I felt fine. And as I lay there waiting to go to sleep, I realized that was because I finally knew where I was. Mum hadn't fobbed me off or told me lies. Jake might have told me that I needed to 'grow up' (and that had *hurt*), but Mum, who knew me far, far better than Jake, was treating me as if I already had. She clearly thought that I was sensible enough to hear the truth.

So I knew what was going on right now, and somehow that seemed enough. It led me on to wondering if Mum felt the same about not knowing what was happening with Laura at Dad's house. Did she think I was keeping things from her?

She'd still be tapping away at work stuff on her laptop. I got up, put on my dressing gown and went downstairs.

'Something else?' 'Something more.'

'Problem?' she said, the way she does, when I came in.

'Not really, no.' I dropped on the sofa and tucked my bare feet under me. 'I was just wondering what was going on with Dad, and wondered if you knew.

She looked up, startled. 'Me? How would I know?'

'Well, you still talk to him.'

'About you. And about arrangements. But not about his private life.'

'Well, I'm confused by it,' I said. 'I mean, here's this new friend of his, this Laura who he met at the mall—'

'I did know that,' she broke in ruefully.

'I'm sorry about that. It was an accident.'

'I know. I know. It wasn't your fault and I shouldn't have brought it up again.'

I pressed on. 'Well, the thing is, I've no idea if that is what she is – just a new friend – or if she's going to turn out to be something else.'

'Something else?'

'Something more.'

'Perhaps your dad's not sure yet, either.'

'No, perhaps he's not. I'm pretty sure he fancies her. He blushes every time her name comes up. But on the other hand, the Hentys know her quite well and—'

She had already interrupted me. 'The *Hentys* know her? How come?'

So I explained. 'She helped Mrs Henty with the foam supports for Andy's bed and wheelchair when he first came out of hospital. And Mrs Henty reckons that she's an angel in disguise who goes around sorting people out. She used to be in Fabrics and Cushions when she sorted out Andy. And now that she's moved to Paints and Wallpapers, she's sorting out Dad. But Alice and I began to wonder if she's going to be my stepmother. And I know she's got twins.'

'Twins? Have you met them?'

'No. I only know that one of them got married. And that their father's family was from the Caribbean, and one of them can whistle.'

She took a moment or two to think about what I had told her. Then she said, 'Well, sweetie, did you want me to ask your father about any of this?'

'Please don't!' I said.

'So you told me because . . . ?'

Her voice trailed off. It suddenly occurred to me that she might think that I was saying all this out of spite. Rubbing it in that she and Richard had ended up on a break, but Dad had found an angel to look after him. That wasn't what I'd had in mind at all. I simply wanted her to understand. She'd treated me as if I were an adult. She had been open. I wanted her to know I could be open in return.

I didn't see how I could explain all that without things getting pretty complicated. I think I lost my nerve. So all I did was untuck my feet and gather my dressing gown more tightly around me.

'No *special* reason,' I said. 'None. But I suppose we live together so I wanted you to know.'

On the way back to my room, I heard myself mutter, 'So sucks yah boo to you, Jake!' It might not have been a very *grown-up* thing to think, but hey! Everyone needs to let their hair down now and again.

Bump in the road

At school next day, I saw Jake eyeing me uneasily across the room. I knew there must be something that he wanted to say, so when the third bell rang and the room cleared, I snapped off a couple of pencil points, and strolled across to use the stupid electric sharpener that barely works, but still sits on the bench beside his desk.

He looked up from packing a heap of scruffy papers into his backpack. 'Hi, Scarlet. How's things?'

'Quiet,' I said, and then to offer him the opening he needed, I added, 'Surprisingly quiet.'

'You mean at home?'

I nodded. 'Yes. How about at your place?'

His look of unease deepened. 'My uncle's been around a whole lot more than usual.'

Time to come out with it. 'I'm not surprised,' I said. 'He and my mum seem to have hit a pretty big bump in the road.'

'What sort of bump?'

He looked so anxious that I reckoned I should make a joke of it. 'I think it was the wrong sort. I think your uncle would have wanted the chance to have a very different sort of bump.'

Jake looked confused. But finally he realized what I meant. He sighed. 'I *knew* that was the problem. I overheard Dad warning him that wanting children of your own is not a feeling that goes away. He said it was all right for your mum because she already had you.' A thought struck. 'Unless, of course, you were adopted anyway?'

It was a question, so I answered it. 'No. I'm not adopted.'

Jake took up his report. 'Dad said to Richard that it might end up mattering to him more than he realized right now, and he should think about it very carefully.'

'That's certainly what he's doing,' I told Jake. 'He's not been around for ages.'

Jake swung his backpack up on his shoulder. 'We ought to go.'

I followed him across the room. Just as we reached the door, he stopped to ask, 'Is your mum very upset? I mean, she isn't *blaming* him, is she?'

'She might be very upset,' I said. 'But I do know she won't be blaming him because Dad's told me how upset she was to find out she was only ever going to have me.'

I was just thinking how good it felt to prove to Jake that I could have a grown-up conversation about this sort of stuff when he went on to blow it. 'Well, I only hope, if he decides the way Dad thinks he will, that he won't throw you and your mother out of the house.'

'Jesus, Jake!'

To do him justice, he did look horrified at what he'd just heard himself say. He even threw out an arm to try to stop me walking past.

Without another word to him, I brushed it off.

All change again!

Alice was nowhere near as shocked as I thought she should have been. 'But Jake was being *nice*! And maybe he's right.'

'Right?'

'You know – that Richard Naylor could ask your mum to

186

leave the house. If they were in love at the start, maybe they didn't bother with any of that legal stuff.'

'If they split up, I doubt she'll want us to stay there.'

'Would she go back to your dad?'

I took a moment to answer. I think I was trying to force myself to think she might, but in the end I did admit to Alice, 'She says the marriage was as good as over anyway.'

'Do you *believe* that?'

Did I?

I tried to act all cool and indifferent. I just shrugged. But Alice must have seen the way my eyes were filling up. 'You ought to ask your dad,' she said. 'I bet a hundred quid your dad would know.'

So next time I saw Dad, I took Alice's advice. I asked him outright. 'Do you think you and Mum will ever pick up again where you left off?'

'What, make up a merry threesome?'

'Why not? We were all right before.'

He made a face. 'I didn't mean a merry threesome with you. I meant, with Richard Naylor.'

'That might not last,' I told him darkly.

Dad gave me a narrow look. 'Cracks in the ceiling, are there?'

'And the walls. His brother's telling him that he'll be miserable if he can't have his own babies.'

He stared. 'Your *mother* told you that?'

'No,' I said. 'Jake let it out. He overheard his dad and Richard talking.'

'Christ! All you children! You've got ears on stalks!'

'We are not *children*,' I informed him. 'Children make dens on the landing and play in sandpits. People like me and Jake and Alice spend our time living with the fallout from people your age's messy, selfish lives.'

He was put out at that. 'Oh, yes?' But you could tell he didn't feel like arguing because he changed the subject back to what I'd told him. 'So does your mother know this?'

'I think so. Yes.'

'And how's she taking it?'

'Seems very calm.'

He sighed. 'Fair play to Fran. Since she's been through the wringer herself on this one, she'll be the first to understand.'

'Dad,' I said. 'If she decides to leave – or if he makes it difficult for her to stay – will you invite her back here?'

He looked a little shifty. 'You mean, for good?'

'If she wants.'

'Treat it all like a hiccup? Pick up the pieces and try to soldier on much as before?'

'That sort of thing.'

He took his time to answer – long enough for me to guess that wasn't what he wanted any more. In the end, all he said was, 'It's been a huge upheaval, Scarlet. Absolutely *huge*. I'm not sure that I could pretend things haven't changed.'

I pushed. 'Because of Laura?'

To my astonishment, he didn't even try to play her down. 'Yes, I admit it. Partly because of Laura.'

So it was him as well as Mum! Both of them coming around to treating me as if I was grown-up enough to know the truth about my own family. I wasn't going to botch things the way Jake had with me.

'Right,' I said. 'All change again! No sweet baby Naylor siblings for me, it seems – just grown-up stepbrothers. One with a wife and one with a piercing whistle.'

Now he was staring at me again. 'Who told you about them?'

I tapped the side of my nose. 'Oh, Alice and I – we have our methods.'

Dad burst out laughing. 'Scarlet,' he said. 'You are *remarkable*.'

'That's what Mum says,' I told him as I ran upstairs.

One step ahead – as usual

I'm not the sort to quit while I'm ahead, so I slid in another question when we'd started supper. 'So what *will* happen if Richard Naylor and Mum split up once and for all?'

He peered at me over the reading glasses perched on

189

the end of his nose. (It was fish curry and he wanted to be sure he'd spot the bones.) 'What do you mean, "what will happen"?'

'Will he chuck us out of the house? Or raise the rent so high that Mum will have to move?'

Dad pushed a sliver of ginger to the edge of his plate. 'Do you remember her signing any lease or anything?'

I leaned across to steal the ginger. 'It's no use asking me. I didn't even realize we were moving there till everything was settled. What worries me is that he'll want to move us back to that flat by the station. That place was horrible.'

'No, that won't happen,' said Dad. 'Your mother has more pride than that. If it gets awkward for you to stay where you are now, she'll find some other place to rent that's nothing whatsoever to do with Richard Naylor.' He raised his eyes to mine across the table. 'In fact, I shouldn't really tell you this, but she's one step ahead.' Ruefully, he grinned. 'As usual.'

'How so?'

'She has been hassling me to get a valuation for this house and pay her off.'

'Pay her off?'

'It was her home as well. For fourteen years. So she's entitled to half of its value.'

'And can you give her that?'

He shook his head. 'No chance. I'd have to sell the place and move somewhere smaller.'

'But you've not had it valued yet?'

'Not yet.'

'Or put it up for sale?'

'No.'

'Why not – if Mum's been hassling you?' A thought struck. 'Is it because you think Laura Deloy might end up living here with you, and that might bail you out?'

He was embarrassed enough to try to wriggle out of the question by answering sideways. 'Scarlet, nobody Laura's age moves in with someone simply to bail them out.'

I watched him lower his head, pretending to look for more fish bones. But this was my life as well. I wasn't going to faff about. 'Dad,' I said sternly. 'Are you really, really soft on her?'

He laid his fork across his plate and looked at me for quite a while. And then he said, 'I might be. Yes, Scarlet. Yes, I suppose I am.'

'Stalemate all round.'

'Stalemate!' said Alice next morning, when I'd cycled over to her house to help her look after Archie. 'Richard Naylor is busy thinking. Your mum's waiting for her share of the house. And your dad's dithering in case he ends up liking

191

Laura enough to ask her to move in, rather than move out himself. Stalemate all round.'

'It can't last very much longer,' I told Alice. 'Dad can't wait for ever to give Mum her share.'

Alice was sniffing the air. 'Is that you, Scarlet? Did you just poo in your pants?'

I came up with the usual response. 'No, Alice. I did not. Maybe you pooed in yours?'

'No. Definitely not me.'

We both stared down at Archie. 'Is it *you*, Archie? Did you poo in your pants? *Again!*'

He crumpled up with laughter. Archie believes that Alice and I are the funniest people in the world.

'Your turn,' I said to Alice.

'No. I changed him only five minutes before you came.'

'You always say that.'

'And it's always true.'

'I suppose I believe that.' I scooped up Archie. On the way to his changing table in the bathroom I called back over my shoulder, 'If everything goes wrong, can I come and live here with you, under your bed?'

'Of course you can. Best mates for ever.'

She probably said more, but I'd already kicked the bathroom door closed behind Archie and me.

I laid him on the padded mat. He reached for my hair. Mine's not as long as Alice's, so it's quite easy to avoid his grabbing fingers. 'OK, Archie. Off with the old and on with the new. Legs up!'

I thought about him all the time that I was changing him. His chubby kicking legs, his flailing arms when he gets cross with being wiped. His lovely soft, pink bum. I love the way he crumples up when we blow raspberries on his bare tummy. I love the way he looks confused whenever we squeeze his toes, as if he still can't work out what's bending them forward and back, and making them tickle. I love the way he finally gives up, and lies there like a tiny lord, accepting the intimate services of his slaves. And how he knows when we're done. He reaches up, and snuggles in. 'Carlit!' he calls me. 'Carlit!'

I changed his nappy and—

It's horrible to say – so disloyal – but I could understand why Richard Naylor had stayed away from us so long, trying to make up his mind.

And I was really hoping he'd make the right decision for himself – and have the sense to dump my mum.

'I overheard the two of them discussing it.'

Alice didn't even seem startled when I came back with our new, sweet-smelling Archie and said, 'Maybe it would be best all round if Richard Naylor decides to stay away.'

She just made space for me and Archie on the bed and said, 'That's certainly what my mum and dad think.'

That got to me. I could just see the Hentys sitting round their supper table, discussing the business as if were some new idea put forward by the council. 'So you've all been talking about it?'

At once she realized that she'd put her foot in it. 'I only told Mum what you told me. And then I overheard the two of them discussing it.'

I wasn't at all sure that I wanted to know. But once Alice had wellied in like that, I found myself having to ask. 'So what were they saying?'

She answered uneasily, 'Well, Mum thinks, if Richard Naylor really does want babies of his very own, then splitting up is for the best. But Dad was arguing that there must be hundreds of couples who fall in love and then find out that one or another of them can't have children. If Richard was really and truly in love with your mum, it shouldn't matter.'

Archie was wriggling towards the edge of the bed. We held onto his grubby yellow bodysuit till he was safely on the floor. 'It might, though,' I reminded her. 'In fact, it clearly does, or he'd be with her right now.' As soon as I was sure that Archie wasn't watching, I passed Alice one of my mints to keep things friendly between us while I asked, 'So what do *you* think? Do you believe the one who turns out not to have the problem should just swan off and leave the other with their rotten luck?'

'It wouldn't be that rotten,' Alice pointed out. 'Plenty of people in the world are adopted, with parents who love them just as much.' She pointed an accusing finger. 'Just look at you and Archie. If my whole family burned up in a fire, you'd snatch him up. You'd love him just as if he were your own. You practically already do! You wouldn't have a problem with him not being truly your baby from the start.'

'No,' I admitted. 'But that would be because things happened to turn out that way. If people marry and then find out they can't have babies, they can at least tell themselves they ended up like that by chance, and are in it together. But Richard took up with my mum before he thought about it properly.' (I nearly said, 'before he met Archie', but that would have made me sound even more weird about Archie than I am.)

'Dad said that *everyone* thinks about whether or not they'll want children.'

I never thought that I would end up sticking up for my mum's boyfriend! 'Well, maybe Richard Naylor did, but not quite hard enough. And now it's come to the crunch he's realized that it won't just be simple bad luck and a horrible surprise if he can't have them. If he stays with my mum, he will have *chosen* it.' I added one more tiny thing in Richard Naylor's defence. 'Maybe the bravest thing for him to do is face how he really feels, and call the whole thing off.'

Stupid little things

I'd hoped we'd leave it there, but Alice is a Henty, and they keep arguing to the bitter end. 'It's not as if there aren't other ways to have a baby, Scarlet. Hormones and stuff. Mum said that working in a hospital, your mother must know how that works. Anyway, there might be new kinds of treatments nowadays that weren't around when she was having you. Maybe she *could* get pregnant.'

'That's not her problem. She can get pregnant. She just can't keep babies going.'

'What about women who have your baby for you? Unless, of course—'

She broke off. Had she just guessed my mother didn't want to go through the bother and expense, and all the awfulness of some of the tests and treatments? And all for someone else's sake, when she already had me. Maybe Alice had come to the same conclusion as I had – that if neither Mum nor Richard loved the other enough to make the sacrifice that one of them would have to make, then it was probably best if they split up.

It would have been all right if Alice had just changed

the subject. Instead, she said, 'Oh, let's just drop it, Scarlet. Whatever happens will happen. Who cares, anyway?'

That did annoy me. *I* care.

'I thought your family must,' I snapped back sarcastically. 'I mean, it sounds as if you've all been spending lots of time chewing it over.'

It was Archie who saved us. His eyes bulged and his cheeks went scarlet. That look of total concentration came over his face and up rose the usual pong.

I sniffed the air. 'Is that you, Alice?' I asked her sternly. 'Did you just poo in your pants?'

She came out with the answer as usual. 'No, Scarlet. I did not. Maybe you pooed in yours?'

We grinned at one another. 'Not me,' I told her. 'And it's definitely your turn to change him this time.'

So we were friends again before she'd even carried Archie out of the room. When we went down an hour later to give him back to Bev, Andy's wheelchair was parked at the bottom of the stairs. Its brakes were on, and inching my way around it, I stumbled on Ben's cycling helmet on the floor. That made me remember what Jake had told me about Alice tripping on her brother's football boot and irritably kicking it out of sight behind the coat rack. I couldn't help it – I shot Alice a sideways glance. Did stupid little things like that always remind her?

No wonder she'd run out of patience with my mum and

Richard's problem. It sounded so unfeeling when she'd said it: 'Whatever happens will happen. Who cares anyway?' But how can you sympathize with people who are still free to make decisions when every day you see the terrible results of something that came totally out of nowhere to change a life in far worse ways?

And for far longer. Probably for ever.

Suppose . . .

That evening, I curled sideways on the cushion in my port-hole window. The moon was scudding in and out behind the clouds, and I was watching the branches sway as fierce spatters of rain kept hitting the panes. I'd wrapped myself in my downie to keep warm, and I think I was enjoying just staring moodily out into the dark, and all that weather.

I know that I was wondering just how much in love with Richard my mother had ever been. Enough to leave my dad, but not enough to want to solve the baby problem? Did something change in between? Or was the very business of her walking out more complicated than I'd realized? Maybe it wasn't easy for her to leave someone as easy-going as my dad, especially knowing she wouldn't just be turning her own life upside down, but mine as well.

Maybe, to do something so drastic, she had to work up quite a head of steam.

I'm sure she would have found it easier if there'd been something pushing her to go. If Dad was a horrible drunk who reeled home every night stinking of booze, snarling and grumbling, she'd soon have made for the door. Or if he'd been a bully – even hitting her – she'd have been crazy not to go at once and take me with her. It wouldn't have been fair to leave me behind to deal with something that she couldn't stand herself.

Suppose he'd been a gambler. That would have made it really easy to leave. Life with a gambler must be *awful*. You waste whole hours in supermarket aisles, working out if this tin of beans is better value than that one, or if it's sensible to buy a jumbo-sized or small loaf. And meanwhile, the person you live with is shovelling all the money you've been scrimping to save, and plenty more besides, into some stupid machine in the hope that a line of oranges or lemons might spin round right to win a jackpot. Or laying a 'dead cert' bet on some horse who might go lame before it reaches the first bend.

No, not for me, I thought. None of them. I wouldn't just walk away. I'd run. Run! Get as far away as I could.

There were other things too, just irritating habits that might get so annoying you'd finally crack. Nagging, say. Just imagine being married to someone who goes on and on at you, telling you what to do, reminding you that you've not done it yet, and, when you do get round to it just to try to shut them up, telling you you're doing it wrong. You expect that sort of thing in school. You get a lot of it from parents. But suppose you married someone who did that all the time? Grim!

Or endless housecleaning – like Mrs Simmons along our road with obsessive compulsive disorder. 'Poor thing,' Mum said. 'She spent all her waking hours wiping and dusting and polishing and scrubbing. Why, even on Christmas morning she'd dust and vacuum the entire house! Her Alan just walked out one day and no one was surprised.'

Dad's not like any of those. There's nothing about Dad (except for being a bit dull) to force you to decide to go. So if there's nothing from inside pushing you to leave, maybe you need some sort of magnet force outside that's strong enough to make you feel you're being dragged away.

Maybe you need to think that you are madly in love.

But, once you were out, you wouldn't need that any more.

It would be safe to think again.

No sign

They tell you nothing. *Nothing*. They're always on about how 'this is a family' and 'we must all give and take' and 'be aware of the needs of other people'. But all that stuff's a one-way street. Unless you as good as skewer it out of them, they tell you *nothing*.

So, was Mum sadder than before, with Richard no longer about? Or happier? I couldn't tell. To me, she seemed the same as ever – busy with phone calls from work, a bit distracted, quick to be snappy and bossy. 'Did you bring down that dirty laundry, Scarlet?' 'If you've time to sit texting, I take it you've finished your homework.'

You know the sort of thing. Perfectly normal.

More days passed with no sign of Richard Naylor. I was so curious I asked her what was going on. I waited till she had her hands deep in the sink, washing her best cashmere top, and then I said, as meekly as I could without her instantly getting suspicious, 'Mum, do you think Richard might be coming round this week?'

I don't know what I thought she might reply – apart, of

course, from throwing a question back at me. And that's exactly what she did. 'Why do you ask?'

'Oh, only because we haven't seen him for so long,' I answered casually. 'I think he must have forgotten he's my unofficial Maths tutor.'

She turned from the sink. 'Are you in trouble with the homework, Scarlet? Because if you are, you ought to phone him. He'd be happy to explain.'

'It was a sort of *joke*,' I said. And then I pounced. 'I was just wondering if you had dumped him.'

I saw her face sort of stiffen, then she said, 'Not quite.'

'Not quite?'

She turned back to her soapy bowl. 'I will be honest with you, Scarlet. I had a talk with Richard about how I saw the two of us having a future together. And now he's thinking about things.'

She leaned over the soggy lump of cashmere in the sink to hide her face. But she was trapped. If she walked off now, it would look too obvious. So I pursued it. 'And are you supposed to be thinking about things as well?'

She sounded a little shocked. 'Me? What do *I* have to think about?'

'The same as Richard? Babies?'

'For God's sake, Scarlet!' she snapped. 'I'm over *forty*. I told you. I'm not going to start on all that business again.'

'But people your age do.'

'Well, more fool them!'

Yes. That is what she said. 'Well, more fool them!'

'Whose baby *is* this, anyhow?'

It was Alice who spotted him. Richard was outside the supermarket, gripping a couple of overflowing bags. I didn't
notice till Alice suddenly took off with Archie in the stroller
to cut him off outside the shoe repair place, beside the double
doors. 'Hi, Richard! Say hello to Archie! Archie, look! It's
the kind man who lets you pull his hair.'

I could have killed her. I'd told her exactly what Mum
said only a few days before. She couldn't possibly have
forgotten.

Richard dropped to his knees in front of Archie and let
go of his over-full bags. One or two things spilled out, but
apart from stopping them roll too far away from him, he
didn't seem bothered. 'Hi, Archie! How's life with you these
days?'

'Dada!' said Archie, holding out his arms.

Oh, brilliant. Just what we needed . . .

'He doesn't mean that,' I said hastily. 'Archie says Dada
to pretty well every man he meets.'

'Don't tell me that,' said Richard. 'I was feeling flattered.'

He stretched out a finger to press Archie's nose, and said to me and Alice, 'OK then, you two. Time to come clean. Whose baby *is* this, anyhow? Is he yours, Alice? Or is he Scarlet's? Because you two spend so much time with him that I'm beginning to believe there is a mystery here. You claim there's such a person as "Archie's mum", but I suspect she's one of you two.' He beamed at Alice. 'Spit it out, Alice. Is he yours? Or are you covering up for Scarlet?'

He looked from Alice to me. I was about to take control of the stroller and mutter something about getting Archie back, when Alice said, 'So which of us do *you* think he belongs to?'

I turned to stare. Alice was flirting with him *again*.

'I think it's you,' he said, grinning at Alice. 'I reckon Scarlet here has far more hard sense than to let a baby interfere with her life.' I sensed he was about to add, 'Just like her mother.' But, to be fair to him, he stopped right there.

'Babies don't interfere,' said Alice. 'Babies are *lovely*. And you know that. Look at you. You've only met Archie a couple of times, and see how soft on him you are already.'

'All *too* soft,' Richard told her ruefully.

A woman driving a green car flashed her lights as she cruised round the corner. I turned to see whose attention she was trying to catch, but there was no one behind us.

Alice said boldly, 'Would you really like to have a baby like Archie?'

Richard's colour rose. He stared at Alice, then his voice dropped to a mumble. 'Not sure this is a conversation that we should be having.'

I couldn't believe what Alice dared to say to him next. 'Well, I certainly hope that, whatever it is that you're thinking about babies, Scarlet's mum knows.'

Now you could tell that he was really irritated. 'That's not your business, Alice,' he told her crisply. 'But, as it happens, yes, she does.'

The green car drew up beside us and you could see it on his face: Rescue! Here comes the cavalry! The woman leaned across to call through the window, 'Richard, the boot's unlocked. Or you can just dump the bags on the back seat.'

Richard bent to press Archie's nose again, then scrabbled for the things that lay around him. 'Bye, girls!' he said. 'Bye, Archie! Be good!'

And, in a flash, he'd thrown himself into the passenger seat, and they were driving away.

'Not just like that! Not here!'

The moment the car moved off, I turned on Alice. 'Why did you *do* that?'

She stared at me. 'Do what?'

'Ask him those horrible, nosy, personal questions! *Grill* him, as if you were Bicky and hadn't any idea when to stop!'

She shrugged. 'If you don't ask, they never tell you anything. You know that.'

And I did know that, having ambushed Mum exactly the same way while she was rinsing out her cashmere top. But Mum at least is *family*. 'You pushed your luck,' I told Alice, 'going on at him like that. I'm not surprised he told you where to get off.'

Alice was unrepentant. 'You had to take your mum by surprise. Why shouldn't you know what's going on in his mind as well as hers? You live with her in his house, after all.'

'Not all the time.'

She scoffed at that. 'Enough of it! So what the two of them decide will make a difference in your life. Why should you hang around, just wondering what the end game is going to be, till one of them finally bothers to bring you up to date? Why shouldn't we ask?'

'Not just like that!' I said. 'Not here! Outside a supermarket.'

'Why not? He was here. We were here.' That reminded her. 'And who was that who picked him up? Do you suppose it was some brand-new girlfriend?'

'Now you are really losing your grip,' I said. 'That would have been Jake's mum.'

'Jake's mum?'

'Yes, she's his sister-in-law.'

'What makes you so sure of that?'

'Her car,' I said. 'It was a safe old boring parent car.'

Alice thought back. 'You're right. A girlfriend wouldn't drive a car like that.'

Archie began to fuss just then, so we pushed on.

'Sorry? Alice said *what*?'

It was the worst mistake, my telling Mum about us bumping into Richard. I only did it because I was still so fed up with Alice – not quite enough to sulk at her while we took Archie home. (She wasn't in the best of moods herself – I'd made a big mistake comparing her to Bicky.) But more than fed up enough to want Mum to agree with me that what Alice said to Richard had been way out of line.

I wasn't sure that Mum was paying much attention at first. But then she swung round from her computer screen. 'Sorry? Alice said *what*?'

I told her again.

'To Richard? You two bumped into him outside the supermarket, and Alice came out with that? But *why*?'

I shrugged. 'I don't know. Probably because we'd been talking about it.'

That didn't go down well. Her tone was frosty. 'Oh, *had* you?'

I tried to backtrack, fast. 'Well, only a bit.'

'But clearly enough for Alice to ask him, first if he really wanted babies of his own, and then if he had shared his feelings with me?'

I could tell Mum was fizzing with resentment. I'd started off wanting to share my irritation with Alice. But all of a sudden I was regretting saying anything about it to Mum. Alice and I have been best mates for years. I didn't want my mother spinning into a giant huff each time she saw her.

'I don't think Alice meant what she said to come out sounding quite as nosy as it did.'

That didn't calm Mum down. 'And how else would it sound?' she snapped. 'Not to mention the fact that nothing between Richard and myself is anything to do with Alice. None of it!'

She was so angry she had risen from her chair.

Who needs a row if they can wriggle out of it? 'I know that,' I said. 'That's what I told her. But I think Alice had been thinking about it quite a bit, and what she thought just popped out when we saw him.'

She wasn't buying that. She went all hoity-toity on me. '*Why* was she thinking about it? How much time have the two of you spent discussing my affairs?'

'It wasn't *me* that set her off.'

Mistake! Even as I came out with it, alarm bells rang. But it was too late.

'Really? Not you? Then who?'

I held off answering, hoping she'd go off on another tack. But I could see she wasn't going to leave it. She took a couple of steps towards me. 'Who, Scarlet? You tell me! Now! If it's not you who's been discussing the details of my private life with Alice, then who is it?'

I was an idiot. I thought if I brought adults into it, she might back off. 'I think that Alice heard her mum and dad discussing it.'

'Alice's mother and father?' Her eyes flashed. 'Talking about my private life in front of Alice?'

There was no going back. 'I'm sure they didn't know that Alice was listening. I think they thought the problem was quite complicated. They wouldn't have been nasty, I'm sure. They're not like that. I expect they were just discussing what was the best thing to do.'

Her voice dripped with scorn. 'Oh, very kind of them, I'm sure!'

I don't know why I bothered to keep on. I might have known that I was in for it. 'And Alice felt the same. She just felt sorry for you. And for Richard.'

I'd clearly put my foot in even deeper. No one likes being pitied. There was the iciest silence. Then, 'I think you'd better

209

leave the room,' Mum said, as if she were some snotty queen and I were just a grubby little palace maid whose shoes had left a trail of mud over her royal carpets. 'And please make sure that Alice doesn't show up on my doorstep. The girl clearly has no sense whatever of other people's privacy. I'd rather that she stayed away.'

And, just like that, Mum turned her back on me.

'What scarlet book?'

I wasn't going to be ordered out like that. Why should I? I was *furious*. 'It isn't just *your* doorstep,' I reminded her. 'I live here too! And if I want to have my best friend over, you can't stop me.'

Mum was still acting snotty. 'I'm very sorry, Scarlet. But I don't choose to have anyone in my house who has so little sense of other people's personal privacy.'

See? *Her* doorstep. And now *her* house. She wasn't even *listening*. 'It's *not* just your house!' I shouted. 'And as for privacy and people being nosy, I don't know how you have the *nerve*. What about *you*?'

'What *about* me?'

'The scarlet book,' I sneered.

She acted totally baffled. 'What scarlet book?'

That really did annoy me. 'What scarlet book? You know what scarlet book! I'm talking about the book you gave me with the blank pages. That wasn't a proper gift. I know what that was about. All you wanted to do with that was tempt me into writing about my feelings so you could sneak into my room at any time you liked, and nose through to find out what I was thinking!'

She looked at me as if I was unhinged. 'That is such nonsense!'

'Oh, is it?' I practically screamed at her. 'Oh, is it really?'

She put on that 'I'm a calm grown-up and you're an over-excited child' tone of voice. 'Scarlet, I gave you that book because I thought you'd *like* it. I truly don't understand what more you're trying to make of it.'

I was still yelling. 'Oh, don't you, Mum! I think you do!'

She'd had enough. Her own voice rose. 'You watch your tone with me!'

But I had totally lost it. 'Well, you watch yours with me! I live here too. I have a life as well. And I've a right to talk to my best friend about the things you do, since pretty well everything affects me as much as it does you. More, some-times!' I was so *angry*. 'And if you can't see that, then maybe I shouldn't be here!'

'Scarlet, if this is the way you're going to behave . . .'
She broke off.

Oh, didn't I have her then! '*What* were you going to say?'

She had the grace to blush. 'Nothing. I wasn't going to say a thing.'

I wasn't going to let it go. 'Oh, yes you were. You were about to say that, if this is the way I'm going to behave, then maybe I'm right and I *shouldn't* be here. Well, don't think for a single moment I want to stay where I know I'm not wanted.'

I think that she began to panic. 'Don't be so silly, Scarlet. Of course you're wanted!'

But I'd gone far too far to back down now. 'No. I don't think I am! I reckon I'm only welcome if I go around thinking exactly what you want me to think, and making sure I don't talk to my friends about anything important. I'm only welcome if I go round like some dumb goody two-shoes who lets things happen round her but never has her own opinions. Well, if that's the only thing that suits you, I can tell you right now that I'd rather live at Dad's house!'

'Scarlet—'

Whatever she was going to say, I didn't let her. With one last parting shot, I slammed the door behind me.

'And I'm off there right now!'

'No problem. I'm just staying here.'

I don't think Dad realized at first that I'd come round in any different way from usual. When I walked through the door, he only said, 'Hi, pumpkin. I wasn't expecting to see you till Friday.'

I dumped my overflowing school bag on the floor. 'Well, here I am.'

'Your mother knows you're here?'

I felt quite smug as I said it: 'She certainly ought to, because I did tell her.'

I didn't say another word about the blow-up – just lugged my stuff upstairs. But by the time I came down again, it was quite obvious that either she had been in touch with him, or he had checked with her.

'So what's this problem, Scarlet?'

'No problem,' I said coolly. 'I'm just staying here.'

'Till things calm down?'

I didn't want a lecture or an argument, so I just shrugged.

He tried again. 'You know your mother isn't at all happy about this?'

I snapped, 'Not top of my boo-hoo list,' and he left it

there. I suppose he thought that it was best to keep off my back till I'd had time to think. He shared the supper he'd planned, and put out cheese and biscuits to make up for our measly helpings. We watched the first half of a boring film before I made an excuse to go upstairs to tell Alice what had happened.

I heard him tap on my door as he went past. 'Sleep tight, Scarlet!' And by the time that my alarm went off in the morning, he'd gone to work.

While I was on the way to school, Mum sent me several texts, but I ignored them all. I was still furious. Alice had taken my side the night before and told me that she thought my mum was totally in the wrong. I worried that she might be saying that because she secretly felt bad that what she'd said had started all this trouble. But Alice reminded me that while she was practically living with us all the time that Andy was in hospital, we'd more than once overheard my parents talking about her family and how they were coping. She hadn't thought that they were being nosy. She'd just assumed that they were worrying because they *cared*. So every time I remembered another quite unreasonable thing that Mum had said, Alice had chimed in: 'Bit hypocritical!' or, 'Doesn't she think that we should even *talk*?'

I skipped lunch – slid out of the faulty fire door, and went back home to pack a wheelie bag with more things I'd need. I shoved shoes and sneakers around the edges, then took the scarlet book out of its hiding place and laid it in the middle. (No way I was leaving that, in case she saw that there was nothing in it. No. Let her sweat!) I emptied the drawer of pyjamas and underwear on top, picked out a few other clothes I like to wear, and forced the rest of my school uniform down into what little space I had left.

By the time I got over to Dad's house, he was already home. At the sight of the wheelie bag, he looked horrified. 'Scarlet—?'

I cut him off. 'Sorry. No time to talk. I have to get back to school.'

I knew he'd grab his keys and say, 'Get in the car.' I thought he might take the chance of the short journey to start on, but he just muttered on about the traffic and whether I'd be late. In any case, I could tell that he wasn't sure of the right way to tackle things. He needed time to think – or another chat with Mum, maybe.

We made it to school in time. (I knew that if I wasn't there for second registration, the office would phone Mum.) As I rushed through the gates, I heard Dad calling after me, 'Scarlet, we will have to talk about this tonight. So don't make any plans.'

'That's fine,' I shouted. 'Bye!'

'Not till she's said she's sorry.'

As soon as school ended, Mum rang me four times in a row. Alice watched me ignore each call. I think she was getting nervous. 'Scarlet, your mum really, really wants to talk to you.'

'Well, I don't want to talk to her. Not till she's said she's sorry.'

'Perhaps she already has. You haven't listened to her messages.'

'I don't need to listen to her messages. I've read her texts. And all they say is, "Scarlet, we have to talk." And I know what that means. It means, "I have a lot of things to say to you, and you'll have to sit and listen."'

'She *might* be feeling sorry.'

'She'll have to do a lot more than feel sorry,' I said fiercely. (I was still furious.) 'She'll have to apologize. And not just one of those weaselly half-apologies about her being "sorry I'm so upset". She'll have to say sorry for her own behaviour and every nasty, unfair thing she said. And she'll have to do it properly.'

'Maybe your dad will secretly invite her round.'

'If he does that,' I told Alice, 'then I'll walk out! And I'll come over to your house.'

Tears

Being angry must really drain your batteries. When I got back to Dad's that evening, I managed to hold it together through supper ('Scarlet, you'll have to talk to her some time.') and through the washing-up ('You know your mother loves you dearly.') and through our saying goodnight ('Won't you just speak to her – just for a minute or two? I'm sure you'd both feel better.').

But even before I'd shut my bedroom door on him, the tears were pouring down. I cried for hours. I felt *horrible*. I kept imagining things – me crossing the school stage to get my certificate on Speech Day, and Mum not being there because she'd asked, through Dad, if I wanted her to come, and I'd said no. Me going off to university, and Mum never, ever even seeing my room.

That sort of thing.

Every third Friday, Dad goes in to work late – something to do with Weuth Pharma's changing shifts – and when I came down next morning, he was still in the house. 'Scarlet, you're pale as a grub. Didn't you sleep at all?'

217

I wasn't going to have him report back to Mum that I was upset. 'No, I slept fine. But I do feel a bit bunged up and shivery.'

'Maybe you're coming down with something.'

'Maybe.'

'I'll ring your mum.'

'No!'

He shook his head. 'Scarlet, you know you have to talk to her some time.'

'I'll talk to her,' I said. 'But only after she's apologized to me for being so unfair.'

'Not sure that's going to happen . . .'

'Fine,' I said. 'I'm happy here – unless I'm getting in your way . . . ?'

'In my way?' The penny dropped. 'Do you mean, with Laura?'

I shrugged. But clearly the idea set him thinking. 'Talking of Laura,' he said, 'do you suppose that it might help if you were to have a little chat with her?'

I stared. 'Why should I chat with Laura?'

'About this problem with your mum,' he said. 'She is a very sympathetic listener. Sensible and kind. You might find, if you talked to Laura about it, that—'

I cut him off. 'Dad! I only got in this because I made the mistake of talking to Mum's stupid boyfriend! Why would I want to take the risk of talking to . . .'

218

I didn't finish up 'your stupid girlfriend'. I checked myself in time and said 'Laura'. But he knew what I'd stopped myself from saying so I expected him to be annoyed.

Instead, to my amazement, he started chuckling. 'Fair point,' he said, and grinned.

If he had wanted me to iron things out with Mum, that was his big mistake. Grinning like that, he'd made it obvious he didn't take the bust-up seriously at all. Even though he had seen me bringing in the wheelie bag, he'd obviously decided that my decision was no more than what he and Mum would call 'teenage dramatics', and I would soon crack and go back.

A *very* big mistake. I hate it when they treat you like a crabby toddler. Especially when you're in the right and they're in the wrong. That made it even easier to ignore all his advice, and Mum's endless calls, and stay the whole of the week. By Friday, though, my mum had clearly had enough. She didn't get in touch again all through the weekend. She simply left a snotty-sounding message with Dad to tell me she was prepared to meet me to discuss what had gone wrong between the two of us 'as soon as I was ready'.

Fat chance. So I stayed round at Dad's the next week too.

Our house again

That following Saturday, Dad prowled around the living room in a strange way for a while, and then said, 'Scarlet . . .'

I looked up. He'd gone pink. 'Scarlet, as it happens, Laura and I had plans to go out tonight. I wondered if you'd like to invite Alice over to keep you company? She can sleep over.'

'I'd like that,' I said. And it was true. It wasn't the idea of having Alice over that pleased me most. She'd come a lot since I moved back. What pleased me most was that I knew I would be able to tell Mum (if I ever spoke to her again) that though she'd said she wouldn't have my best friend Alice over her doorstep, Dad had gone out of his way to invite her into his house.

No. Not into *his* house. Because I wasn't going back. It was *our* house again now. *Ours.*

'Scarlet . . .'

On Monday morning, Jake stepped in front of me as I was chumming Alice along the corridor towards her flute lesson. 'Scarlet . . .'

He looked a bit worked up, but Alice hadn't time to stop and earwig. 'Can't wait. Whenever I'm late, she pays me back by making me play pieces I hate.'

Jake pulled me aside. Luckily no one we knew was walking past because he simply came out with it. 'Mum says your mother has just dumped my uncle.'

Newsflash indeed! And how did I feel about it? Glad, or sorry? But Jake was waiting. 'Has she?' I said. 'For sure?'

'Didn't you even *know*?'

'I've been at Dad's,' I told him to defend myself, and turned to walk back to our home room. Jake fell in step beside me, saying, 'Mum thinks your mum must have given Richard the push. She's certainly warned him that you two are planning to leave his house.'

That irritated me – not what Jake said, but that my mum had said to Richard that the two of us were leaving. I had already *left*.

I still wasn't sure Jake's mum had got things right. 'Wanting to move out might be to do with something else.'

'I doubt it.'

So did I. But I didn't want to talk to Jake about my mum. I fished around for something wishy-washy to say. 'Maybe she worries that she can't pay a proper rent all by herself – not till she's finally sorted things out with my dad.'

'She was quite happy before.'

'That's when she thought . . .'

I broke off. There was no point in going on. The situation was as clear as day, and we were at our home-room door. I said to Jake, 'Well, OK. Maybe they've split up. They never really got it going anyway. He never lived with us.'

'My mother says that Richard was totally in love with her.'

I didn't want to say I thought Jake's mother took a creepily nosy interest in her brother-in-law's life. But I couldn't keep the irritation out of my voice. 'Well, clearly not *enough* in love, because it's turned out that he wants babies of his own more than he wants my mum.'

'He claims she wants not to have any more babies more than she wants *him*.'

'Maybe they're both right,' I said. 'Maybe it's for the best and they have made a sensible, grown-up decision, and Mrs Bennet would be proud of them.'

He glowered at me for a moment, then burst out laughing and we walked into class.

Caller display

Alice had really, really hoped to see Laura on Saturday. (Just being nosy.) But Dad smartened up and left the house at half past six. (Shy.)

He'd only been gone a short while when the landline rang.

Alice was nearer. She reached out to pick it up and hand it over. I stopped her just in time. 'Don't! It might be Mum.'

Alice looked at the caller display. 'You're right.'

We let it ring. It seemed so *loud*. After the room went quiet, Alice said, 'When are you going to speak to her again?'

'When she's said sorry,' I said. 'And she knows that, because Dad's told her.'

'But she still won't?'

'No, she still won't. She says that I have quite as much to apologize to her about as she has to say sorry to me. She's told Dad that she's happy to *talk* to me – she *wants* to talk to me and sort it out – but she's not going to . . .'

I stopped.

'Not going to what?' said Alice.

I felt uneasy even saying it. 'Not going to crawl.'

Neither of us spoke. Then Alice started up again, 'You

don't feel sorry for her enough to make the first move? Even though she's been dumped?'

'She's not been dumped,' I snapped. 'Jake said that Mum dumped Richard. How is it my fault if she falls out with everyone because she always wants things her own way?'

Alice sighed. 'So it's still stalemate between the two of you.'

'Yes, stalemate.'

It was too. I stayed with Dad, and yet another week went past. He made sure to keep Laura well away from me. Mum sent me messages that I refused to answer. And though I know for a fact that Dad suggested it to her, several times, she never once came round.

'Now I've changed my mind.'

Then half term came. We had a whole week off. Dad was at work. He hadn't known in time to get those days as holiday, so I was pretty bored. Alice came round as often as she could between the things her family had already organized. And on the Saturday Mrs Henty took both of us shopping. She bought me a bobble hat with her own money after she'd caught me looking at it wistfully, so when on the drive home she started hinting heavily that Bev could do with a few hours off, I didn't feel that I could be the one to tell her that Alice and I had plans.

We had agreed that we'd be going back to my house because Dad had said that after he finished at the Pill Factory, he would be helping Sajid from work shift something heavy. It would have been a chance to do whatever we wanted without the usual nagging. ('Scarlet! Alice! Think of the neighbours! Turn that music *down*!')

Either Alice forgot, or she was keener than I'd guessed to spend some time with Archie. She didn't argue with her mum, so Mrs Henty turned off at the roundabout to drop us at Bev's place.

I do admit Bev looked *destroyed*. All grey and greasy, with rings under her eyes. She couldn't hand Archie over fast enough. 'You're welcome to him. Since these two back teeth started coming in, he has been *horrible*.'

'No problem,' Alice said. 'Mum says you ought to go to bed and sleep till we get back.'

I didn't get the feeling Bev would need telling twice. We strapped the wailing monster into his stroller, and Alice had to use some force to push him far enough back in the seat for me to fasten the buckles. We tried to ignore his furious struggles and his mighty bawling as we hurried down to the canal, away from all the passers-by who were frowning at us as if his terrible temper was our fault.

'It must be awful, being stared at like that if it's your own baby,' I admitted. 'At least these people must surely realize that Archie isn't ours.'

'I nearly stuck my tongue out at that last woman.'

'I wish you had.'

When Archie finally fell asleep, we plonked ourselves down on the very next bench. 'I can see why your mum doesn't want to start all over again,' said Alice.

I turned to grin at her. 'I thought you were the one who reckoned love should conquer all.'

'That was before,' said Alice. 'Now I've changed my mind.'

We sat a little longer. Then Alice said, 'Hey! Do you suppose that when your mother had that horrible go at you, she might have only just decided she couldn't face the whole trying for a baby thing again?'

I thought back to the morning when Jake had stepped in front of me and told me his uncle had been dumped. 'That might fit in.'

Alice was busy working out the timing as well. 'That *would* fit in. If she'd just made up her mind, she might have been feeling awful.'

'I suppose so.'

Alice was still chewing it over. 'Or perhaps she was feeling terrible because it would have been so nice to marry him, and just go on and have a baby with no problem. Like Motty's mum.'

'And Helena's.'

Alice made a face. 'It's horrible, to think your body doesn't work the way it should, so you can't run your life the way you want.'

I'm sure she had Andy in mind. But I thought more about what Dad had said about his feelings, and Mum's, all of those years ago. *Tears ran too deep.* I turned to Alice. 'You really think that that might be what set her off?'

'It might. It probably would me.'

'But not being able to say sorry! That's nothing to do with how it all began. That's just pure stubbornness.'

Alice let out a snort of laughter. 'You can talk, Scarlet!'

'What's that supposed to mean?'

'Just what I said – that when it comes to being stubborn, you'd take first prize. How long have you been holed up with your dad?'

'Nearly three weeks,' I admitted.

'Well, there you are!'

That rattled me – what she'd just said. I didn't want to talk about it till I'd had time to think, so I stood up. 'Come on,' I said. 'I'm getting really cold. We should take Archie out of the wind. Let's go down the back lanes. Sajid's mum's moved into a nursing home and won't come out again, so my dad's somewhere near here helping Sajid clear out her flat. If we can find him, we can cadge enough to go back to that cafe we passed, and get hot chocolate.'

'Good plan,' she said. 'Archie is bound to wake up starving.' So quickly, before he woke, she took hold of the stroller and wheeled it along towards the first of the lanes.

'Surprise!'

The back lanes are all bumpy, with stones and potholes and weird tufts of dried grass. Archie was jolted horribly in the stroller but never woke. 'He could sleep through an earthquake,' Alice said. 'So which way now?'

'I'm pretty sure Dad said she lived along the Astley Road.'

'Down this lane, then.'

Alice peered over the fences as we went along. 'Lovely big houses.'

'They're mostly split into flats.'

Then Alice stopped. She pointed. 'Isn't that your dad?'

It was too. He and Sajid were heaving a giant red sofa out of some wide French doors and down stone steps into a garden. 'Don't shout to him,' I warned. 'If you startle them, they might drop it.' So Alice and I watched quietly over the fence until the two of them had lowered the massive piece of furniture onto the lawn.

'Surprise!' I called.

Dad swung around. 'Scarlet! And Alice! What are you doing round here?'

'Just stalking you and Sajid.'

Dad wiped away the sweat. 'We're nearly done. Thank God.'

'That sofa looks incredibly heavy.'

'If you think that looks bad, you ought to come inside and see the wardrobe we've been leaving till last.'

Alice and I lifted the stroller up the steps and followed Dad and Sajid into the ground-floor flat. It was practically bare. The pictures had been taken off the walls, and if there had been rugs or carpets, they were gone. The place was light and sunny, with golden wooden floors. Alice and I drifted from one room to another, and almost all of them had doors with steps down to the garden.

'It's gorgeous,' Alice told Sajid. 'Your mum will really miss it.'

'She's too far gone for missing things,' Sajid said. 'But she was happy here for a long while.'

'*Anyone* would be happy here.'

Then Alice did a typical Alice thing. She turned to me and said, 'Your mum should rent it, Scarlet. It would be perfect for her.'

'She doesn't need it. She has a house already.'

'Maybe she does right *now*,' said Alice, as if my dad and Sajid weren't standing right beside us, having to pretend not to listen. 'But that's not going to last, is it? Now they've split up, Richard will soon decide he needs full rent. Your mum won't want that. She'd be better off moving in here.' She pointed. 'Look! You could have that room – the one with steps down to that tiny private lawn. That room is lovely.'

'I don't need any room with Mum,' I told her frostily. 'I live with Dad.'

'There you are! Perfect!'

I could tell Dad was really uncomfortable when I said that. And Alice rolled her eyes. She turned to Sajid, changing tack. 'It is the absolutely perfect flat for Scarlet's mum,' she told him. 'Is it for sale?'

Sajid glanced at my dad. I'm sure he thought it was dead rude to talk about what would be perfect for my mum when the husband she'd left was standing there having to listen. But he did have to answer Alice one way or another, and in the end he said, 'We'll certainly be renting it out for a while. And then, yes, it will probably go up for sale.'

'There you are!' Alice turned back to me. 'Perfect! Ring your mum now. Tell her to come and look.'

'I am not phoning her, and that is that,' I said.

It was Dad who came to the rescue. 'Alice!' he scolded.

'Maybe Sajid doesn't fancy having someone look around the place right now. He may have other plans.'

Sajid was torn. You could tell that he thought Dad might be embarrassed at the whole idea of Mum strolling in. But on the other hand he knew he might be doing everyone a favour. Alice was right. The flat was ideal for Mum, and Sajid might even be thinking that if Mum moved out of Richard Naylor's house, there was more chance that she and Dad would get together again. And he did want a tenant. So after this great yawning pause, he turned to Dad and muttered, 'What do you reckon, Tony? This one is up to you.'

And guess what happened. Dad tried to pass the big decision on to me. 'Scarlet?'

I wasn't having that. 'It's nothing to do with me,' I said. 'I won't be here.'

Alice is like a ferret when she gets started. 'Oh, come on, Scarlet! This place is *lovely*. Perfect for your mum.'

She didn't dare add, 'And for you.'

I gave a 'whatever' shrug.

Alice persisted. 'So she can come and take a *look*.'

'I don't care what she does.'

'All right,' said Alice. 'Phone her.'

I wasn't having that. I turned to Dad. '*You* phone her.'

Dad shook his head. 'No, Scarlet. This is your job.'

'Well, I'm not doing it.'

Then Alice interfered *again*. 'Don't be so silly, Scarlet! Your mum *needs* this flat. You don't have to live here with her. But if she doesn't end up seeing it, you're going to feel horrible each time we go down Astley Road.' She pulled her phone out of her pocket. 'If you don't ring her, I will.'

I snatched the phone from her. 'She's *my* mum! Don't you *dare* phone her!'

'All right. You do it then,'

I gave her such a scowl I am surprised she didn't shrivel into ashes on the spot. 'All right!' I snarled. 'I'll do it.'

And I did.

'I have to tell you something.'

I shut the door between the room I would have chosen to be mine, and everyone else. I didn't want the others listening. And I was all set to cut off the call the moment Mum turned nasty. In fact, I was really, really hoping she'd put a foot wrong right away, so I could just hang up.

I could tell she was startled to hear my voice. 'Scarlet? Is that you?'

'Yes, it's me. I have to tell you something.'

She sounded wary. 'Go on.'

'There is this flat,' I said. 'It used to belong to Sajid's

mum but she's moved out now.' I tried to sound all cool and distant. 'And Dad and Sajid and Alice are here, and they all think you ought to come and see it.'

She sounded even more cautious now. 'Because . . . ?'

I thought, for heaven's sake, stop pussyfooting! But I meant that for me as much as her. 'Because it's lovely!' I burst out. 'It's light and sunny, with wide French doors down to a lovely garden. And Sajid wants to rent it out before he sells it. And we all think it would be absolutely perfect.'

'For us?' she said, as if it never had occurred to her that I would not be coming home to her again some time.

I might have been halfway to being ready to admit I thought that was a possibility. But Mum had the sense not to force me to say it. She broke into the silence she'd just left. 'So should I come to look at it right now?'

Oh, go on, Scarlet, I thought. Just *say* it. 'I think that you should.'

I felt a huge rush of relief. I was so pleased. I hadn't realized, till she had said, 'For us?' how cold and horrid the last weeks had been. And though I'd been determined not to be the first to speak, it had been easy. I was quite sure that Mum would want to talk about how things had gone wrong some time. She always does. But I could tell that she had been as glad as me to let it go right then.

I realized she was saying something else.

'Sorry? I didn't catch that.'

'I said, how did you know that I was looking for another place?'

'I didn't,' I admitted. 'But Alice thought you would be.'

'Oh, Alice!' she said, and laughed. 'Typical Alice.' And I knew from the way that she was saying it that things were going to be all right between the two of them as well.

'Well done.'

The moment Dad and Sajid had heaved the massive wardrobe onto the trailer that Sajid had hired, Dad wanted to go. He was determined not to be around when Mum arrived. 'Want a lift home, Alice?'

I knew that she was keen to stay and see what happened between me and Mum. But Archie had been away from Bev for ages, and he was making all those funny jerks and squeaks that mean he's waking up.

'Oh, please!'

Dad gave me a long hug. 'Well done,' he whispered in my ear. Then he stepped back to unlock Archie's car seat from the stroller frame and carry it out to the street. Alice went after him, wheeling the empty base. We heard the car start up. Sajid and I sat peacefully on the steps together, gazing out at the garden. I didn't want to interrupt his thoughts, so I stayed very quiet till Mum came.

She absolutely loved the place from the moment she walked in. 'I hadn't thought of moving out of where we are so soon,' she told Sajid. 'But it's a wonderful flat. Perfect!' She gazed out through the French doors for the umpteenth time. 'And that's the prettiest garden.'

'My mother was extremely happy here,' Sajid said again.

Mum wandered around the flat once more. Before she went back to the living room to speak to Sajid, she waved me away into the room I guessed would be mine. 'What sort of rent were you—?' I heard her start to ask as she shut the door between us.

Another time, I would have stayed right by the door to listen. But I knew things were going to work out. I slid my back down the wall till I was sitting staring out of the glass door that led to my particular corner of the garden. You could tell someone had deliberately designed it to look tangled and wild. Creepers with purple flowers tumbled around the doorway. Blossoms cascaded over the fence at the side. Bright shrubs and flowers crowded round the tiny patch of lawn that would be mine, all mine. A sort of private, hidden dell. I had a sudden image of myself, flat on my stomach out there in sunlight, writing – not page after page of poisonous resentment in the scarlet book, but something light and cheerful. It was the oddest feeling, and sent me back to thinking about the first time I had settled in my little porthole window in Richard Naylor's house.

It hadn't been that long ago – weeks rather than months. So many changes. For me. For Mum and Dad. And now another change was coming. I could tell Mum had instantly decided to make the move. She wouldn't want to stay in a house that had a really low rent only because the owner had thought that he'd be moving in as well. Jake's uncle was a nice man. He probably wouldn't have rushed to say he would be forced to think again about my mother's payments.

But she wouldn't wait till then. She had her pride. Now that she knew that she and Richard weren't going to stay together, she clearly wanted to leave. It wouldn't be Mum's style to hang around, making the most of living in the bigger place till he said something to her.

I wasn't in the least surprised when she tapped on the door. 'All sorted, Scarlet. Ready to go?'

All sorted? I knew that she could only mean one thing. 'We're taking it?'

'We are.'

Sajid looked just as happy. I suppose, if he was busy moving his mum into a nursing home, then renting out the flat so easily to someone he knew and trusted was good for him as well.

'I'll need to give the bigger bedroom a lick of paint before you move in,' he said. 'It looks pretty awful behind where that great wardrobe stood.'

'Oh, we'll do that,' said Mum. She winked at me. 'Scarlet and I know who to go to for the exact matching shade of paint.'

'Good plan!'

I didn't go back to Mum next day, but we did meet for lunch at Pizza Palace. Everyone around us was being so cheerful and noisy that it was hard to get too deeply into what had gone wrong. She said she had been feeling dreadful about treating me as if I had no business talking about her life with my best friend. I said that I was sorry I hadn't answered her calls.

I was about to go on and tell her I now thought I knew why she'd been feeling particularly sensitive that day, when suddenly she raised her head from shoving all the green olives that she doesn't like to the side of her plate, and said, 'Oh, really, Scarlet! It's been a horrible three weeks without you. Absolutely horrible! I don't think I can bear to pick it all over right now. Shall we put the whole mess to one side and talk about it some other time?'

'Good plan!' I said, guessing – and hoping – that some other time would probably be never.

I moved the stuff I'd taken over to Dad's house back the

next night. Dad heaved the wheelie bag into the boot and drove me. When Mum invited him in for a drink, he followed her into the kitchen. I didn't know if he'd come in to make it easier for me to slide upstairs and empty the bag without Mum hovering, or if he was just being polite.

Or what.

He stayed about forty minutes. When I came down, they seemed to be getting on well enough together. He was catching her up with what the Maddoxes next door were doing about their massive rhododendron and she was even managing to show some interest.

After he'd left, she handed me one of those lovely, smelly bath bombs. 'A welcome home gift!' she said. 'And I was wondering if you would like to come with me tomorrow to Hatcher's Cross. I'm going to match up that paint.'

'We don't have to buy the paint there,' I told her. 'Laura Deloy doesn't need to know we're decorating a room. We could buy it anywhere.'

'No,' Mum said. 'Frankly, I'm glad to have the excuse to bump into her again. I've been uncomfortable about the way we met before.'

'That wasn't your fault.'

'Maybe it wasn't. Still, if she's going to get together with your dad . . .' She paused. 'Even if they're just going to be friends, I'd rather that she saw the better side of me.'

The better side

The better side of me. It was an odd expression, but I thought I knew exactly what she meant. And in my lovely, long, deep, perfumed bath, I thought about it some more. I reckoned that, if I was going to be fair, I'd have to say the grown-ups in my life were mostly trying hard. They'd turned things upside down. But every single one of them seemed to be doing their very best to act like decent human beings. I thought about people in class. I know that some of them – like Jake and Alice and Willow and Pedro – would try to be like that. They wouldn't ever let themselves make anybody's problem worse, just to indulge themselves.

But Bicky and Marina – or even Greg? I wouldn't trust them not to make a bigger deal than they need of an emotional mess. I could see any one of those three enjoying feeling martyred, or stirring things up, even when they could see it made life difficult for other people they might claim they cared about. I wouldn't want to try and get divorced from Marina! Or be any child of Bicky's, when she's so childish herself.

I sloshed about in my delicious scented water, and for the

first time I admitted to myself that Dad and Mum, and even Laura and Richard, had mostly done their very best to make things easier for me.

With luck, I thought, things won't turn out too badly.

'There she is now.'

Of course, when we reached the paint aisle the next afternoon, Laura was nowhere in sight. But it was clear Mum wasn't going to miss out having a word with her if she could help it. As soon as I had pointed out the office on the level above, she started for the spiral stair.

When she came down, she was smiling. 'It seems Laura's on her break. They say that she'll be back in twenty minutes, so we haven't wasted the journey.'

'We wouldn't have wasted the journey anyway,' I reminded her. 'We're here to get matching paint.'

Mum clearly didn't want to hang around the paint aisle. Preferring her meeting with Laura to look dead casual, she steered me over to the bathroom fittings. Together we milled about the shower heads and plugs and mixer taps I'd wasted my time on before. Mum kept up a constant chatter. 'Oh, look at this!' 'My heavens, what a price!' 'That is so ugly. I wonder who on earth would choose a tap like that?' It was clear she was nervous, and it must feel weird to hang around a giant shop, waiting to 'happen to bump into' your husband's new girlfriend so you can put yourself out to be pleasant, and try to get her to forget how rattled and testy you had been the first time the two of you met.

I was so glad when I could tap Mum on the arm and warn her, 'There she is now.'

Mum swung round. 'Where?'

I pointed. 'Laughing with that guy with the straw hair.'

Mum waited till he'd gone. Then she took off towards Laura. I didn't know whether or not I was supposed to follow, but in the end I did because I was so curious. By the time I caught up with her, Mum had introduced herself and it was obvious that Laura remembered her clearly. 'Of course! It was Tony's birthday.'

Mum beamed. 'And you had bought him the most beautiful cake!' She laid a hand on my arm. 'You know Scarlet, of course, Laura. But sadly, you and I never met properly. I was in such a mad hurry that afternoon. I can't remember exactly what it was . . .'

'You said it was a problem at the hospital.'

'Did I? Well, so it would have been. But I was sorry we didn't get to spend a little time getting to know one another. I had to rush off so quickly I must have seemed practically *rude*.'

Nice one, Mum.

You could tell Laura didn't believe a word of it. But you could also tell she wasn't in the business of making an awkward meeting even worse. 'Oh, not at all! Tony explained that you have the most responsible position. He said that hospital can barely run without you.'

'Did he say that?'

'He did.'

'That's very nice of him. But there you go. He is the nicest of men.'

'He certainly is.'

And that was just about the end of it. They stared at one another for a moment or two, with rather fixed smiles on their faces. Then, clearly reckoning she'd done the best she could to redeem herself, Mum moved on to the subject of paint. 'What we *need*, Laura . . .'

And I wandered away.

Just thinking

As we turned off the main road into our own street, Mum glanced across and told me, 'You've been very quiet.'

'I was just thinking.'

'Not about colours, I hope. I did promise Sajid we'd only get a shade that matched.'

'No, not about colours.'

'What, then?'

I thought I might as well come out with it. 'Actually, about Dad and Laura. I was just wondering – if they don't make a go of it . . .'

I didn't need to finish.

'Whether your father and I would get back together again? Is that the question?'

I grinned. 'Just checking.'

'Well,' she said with a hint of irritation, 'it's the same answer as before. No, we would not.' She turned into the driveway and switched off the engine. Then she said, 'What life breaks sometimes has to stay broken, Scarlet. Your dad's a good and steady man. And I don't think I made too bad a stab at being his wife. But that's all over now. I don't think I would ever want to go back to that life.'

She was opening the car door. It was my last chance to push. 'Even for my sake?'

I don't think she could tell from my tone of voice whether I truly meant it, or if it was a joke. But she just told me firmly, 'No. Not even for your sake, sweetpea. And you will survive.'

'Can I borrow you?'

Next morning, Alice stepped in front of Jake the moment he came in the home room. 'Jake, can I borrow you after school?'

In front of everyone, he flung himself onto his knees at her feet. 'What for, my love? A quick romantic fling? Advice on the poetry homework? Help getting the lid off a jar?'

She pulled him up. 'I'll tell you later.'

'Righty-ho. But I will have to be home by six because it's drama club night.'

'That's sort of what it's about.'

As soon as we were in line to go to Assembly, I asked her, 'So what's with you and drama club? Are you thinking of joining?'

'No. It's about Andy. Mum says we have to get him back to doing things, and Jake's the only one I know who still goes every week.'

I'd almost forgotten that Andy had ever acted; it had been so long. I could imagine how he would have lost his confidence, knowing he still couldn't even move on and off the stage without his wheelchair or those clumsy crutches.

244

Still, at least it was possible. Not like aiming to join the football team again right now.

Alice was talking again. 'You'll have to be there as well. I'll have to tell Andy you and Jake were walking home together, otherwise Andy is sure to guess that Mum wanted Jake to come.'

I would do anything for Andy. 'Fine by me.'

Even before school was over, I'd rung Dad to tell him I'd be late: 'I have to help Alice with something.' Jake walked his bike beside us along to the Hentys' house.

'Remember,' Alice warned, 'Andy is really sensitive about what he can and can't do. He mustn't guess that Mum and I have anything to do with this.'

'OK,' said Jake. He followed Alice into the house and gazed around. 'Where is he, anyhow?'

Alice pointed. 'In there.'

Jake tapped on the door, and then we all went in the room. Andy was sitting on the bed, propped up against the pillows, dressed, but not doing anything. His laptop was closed. The lamp we'd bought him for his birthday was on his bedside table, but not on.

'Hi, mate,' said Jake. 'Busy?'

Andy just made a face.

'I'll cut to the chase,' said Jake. 'I have been ordered round to get you back to drama club.'

Knee-deep in corpses

For heaven's sake! Alice and I exchanged looks of despair. How badly could Jake go about the task? Had he forgotten his orders?

Apparently not, because he pedalled on. 'Mrs Philips says that we need you. She can't wait any longer. She says you have to come back now.'

We all three watched as Andy scowled. 'Oh, yes? And how?' He waved one hand at the wheelchair parked on one side of the bed, and the other at the crutches leaning against the wardrobe.

'Either of those will do,' said Jake unsympathetically.

Andy changed tack. 'So why does Mrs Philips want me back so suddenly?'

'Nothing sudden about it,' Jake told him. 'She's been wanting you back for weeks. But now it's turned critical and you *have* to come.'

Andy still sounded downbeat. 'Why? Have you chosen a murder mystery? Need a stage knee-deep in corpses? I suppose Mrs Philips reckons I can at least manage that.'

'Good parts, those,' Jake argued. 'Don't knock 'em.

Not too many lines to learn. But actually she needs your wheelchair skills. Last week she suddenly decided to see if we could do some weird stage version of *X-Men* a friend of hers has written.'

Alice and I exchanged exasperated looks. An *X-Men* play? How did Jake think that he was ever going to get away with that?

But we'd not reckoned with the acting skills that he's picked up along the way. Now he was sounding quite peeved. 'So Mrs Philips tried to give the Professor X part to me but I kept tumbling off the stage. Bruised myself really badly.' He started rooting up his trouser leg as if to exhibit the damage, then let the trouser leg fall. 'So shall I get my dad to pick you up at ten to seven? Wheelchairs fold up, don't they? Will we be able to fit it in the boot?'

'Yes,' Alice told him firmly. 'It folds up brilliantly.'

'Right, then,' said Jake. 'See you at ten to seven, at your gate. You're not to let us down. You're certainly our only hope for trying out this *X-Men* thing for Mrs Philips's friend, and Mrs Philips says she needs you back in any case for *Mamma Mia!*, which we're doing next.'

He turned and winked at Alice as he left. I followed him into the hall, and out of the front door.

'Brilliant!' I told him.

Jake took a bow. 'Just *acting*, Scarlet. What you and Alice wanted.'

I was still anxious. 'But what'll happen when Andy gets there and finds out you were making all that *X-Men* wheelchair stuff up?'

'He won't have time to sulk. We're really short of people for *Mamma Mia!*'

'And it won't be a problem, him finding it quite hard to get about without the crutches?'

'For Pete's sake, Scarlet! Andy can still *act*. He can still *sing*. Everyone has to pitch in. Why, when Mark Wilcox broke both legs—'

I didn't hear the rest about Mark Wilcox, because Jake had swung his own leg over the bike, and was already away.

'Your boyfriend, not mine.'

By the time I came back to Mum's house, two nights later, she had phoned Richard to tell him we'd be leaving the flat.

'Did he mind?'

'I think he was relieved.'

I laid a hand across my brow. 'Farewell, my A in Maths!'

She gave me quite a searching look. 'You don't mind, do you?'

'Moving to the new flat? Why should I mind? It's lovely.'

She brushed that response away. 'No, silly! Me splitting up with Richard. For good.'

'He was *your* boyfriend, not mine.'

'Yes. Stupid of me.' She lifted her hand to her head as if her thoughts were spinning. 'And that flat is a dream. It does solve the problem. I have to say that Richard couldn't have been nicer. He sent his love to you and Alice and Archie, and told me to give you his phone number in case you ever need a bit of help with your Maths.'

'That's good.'

Mum rose from the table. 'The twenty-seventh, I told him. I'm going to have to get on with it if we're to be out of here in time.'

But she's no slouch when she starts on a project. Each time I walked in through the door, something had gone. ('Oh, sorry. That's already packed.' 'I've given that back to your father.' 'Oh, did you *want* it? I could nip down the charity shop and buy it back.')

We had exams, and so the last two days came round so fast it took me by surprise. I'd spent a couple of nights at Dad's, and when I walked in, Mum was leaning over the sink, looking all hot and sweaty, cursing and fussing.

'What's up?'

'Won't drain! Totally blocked! Just at the wrong time!'

'Have you tried the plunger?'

'Of course I've tried the plunger!'

'And pouring boiling water down?'

'Yes, Scarlet. I've tried that.'

You didn't have to be a mind-reader to realize she was on the edge. At any other time, I might have felt the urge to make her feel guilty for not asking me about the exam I'd just taken. But she looked so frayed and tired that I said instead, 'Shall I ring Dad? He might have some idea.'

She didn't even answer, just turned from the sink. 'I'll have another go at it later. I want to send in a meter reading now, before I forget.'

I carried my bag upstairs, out of the way. When I came down, she was back over the sink, but this time blood from her finger was dripping into the scummy backed-up water.

'What have you done?'

'Stabbed myself with the screwdriver, trying to get into the meter box.'

'You need a special key to open that,' I said. 'I know Dad's got one.'

She lost it. 'Oh, for heaven's sake, Scarlet! "Dad can do this!" "Dad's got a thing for that!" Give it a rest. We're separated! I am on my own!'

She pulled out a kitchen chair and sat down, blood dripping on the table. I went to the cabinet to look for the plasters, but they'd been packed away. Instead I handed her a wodge of paper towel to wrap around her finger.

She sat there quietly for a bit while I said nothing.

A positive joy and an asset

At last, Mum lifted her head. 'All this upheaval!' she said. Her voice was shaky. 'All these *changes*. All these decisions!'

I thought she only had the problems of the house move in mind, but she pressed on. 'All this upsetting your dad, and having to divide the money, and moving twice over already, and now again! And all for nothing, since it didn't work out.' To my horror, she burst into tears. 'Oh, Scarlet! I feel such an idiot! I've been a fool. And I've been a terrible, terrible mum, and pretty well ruined your life! And what for? Nothing!'

I did what she'd have done. I lifted the kettle off its base to make sure there was enough water in it to make tea. And then I flicked on its switch.

'You haven't ruined my life,' I told her. 'Don't say that. For one thing, my life's *not* ruined. Living in two places isn't that bad, after all. Hundreds of people do it. Thousands! Half of the people in my class, for starters.' I ripped more sheets of paper off the kitchen roll and passed them across to her. 'And your life isn't ruined either,' I went on. 'You still have choices, after all. Why, you could even go back and tell

Dad that you think you made a big mistake, before he goes and marries Laura Deloy.'

'I've told you! More than once! I am not going back!'

'Right, then,' I said firmly and calmly. 'So we can move into that lovely flat, and you can start a brand-new life.'

She blotted her tears with one of the squares of kitchen roll I'd given her. 'Yes,' she said. 'That's the way I'll have to go.'

'It won't be that bad,' I said. 'Thousands of people do it. And you'll have me.' Teasing, to try to cheer her up, I added, 'My company's not to be sneezed at, after all. Dad says I'm "a positive joy and an asset".'

She lifted her tear-streaked face, curious. 'Your father said that?'

'He did.' I grinned. 'Though I admit that was only because he'd lost something down the side of the car seat and his hands are so big that he couldn't have got it back without me.'

'Yes, but he's right,' she said. 'He's absolutely right. You have become a positive joy and an asset.'

I thought that was interesting – Dad said he thought I *was* one, but my mum thought I'd *become* one.

I'd have to think about that.

'I really can't help?'

When Dad brought round the key for the meter box, he suggested I spend the night before the move at his place.

I looked at Mum. 'What do you think?'

'It might be sensible,' she said. 'Give me a chance for one last whip round.'

I wasn't going to desert her if she needed me. 'I really can't help?'

She shook her head. 'It might be easier if all your bedding and stuff was already boxed.'

Why should I mind? 'OK, then.'

I ran upstairs, knowing that the most useful thing that I could do was not be in earshot when she put her pride aside and asked my dad to fix the sink.

'Ta-*da*!'

When I walked in for registration, Alice was sitting on my desk. 'Ta-*da*!'

She handed me a box wrapped in shining paper.

'What's this?'

'House-warming present, of course! For tomorrow's big day. Mum says to tell you it's from all of us.'

It was a box of china eggs, all in a china nest. Some of the eggs were creamy-coloured and some were pinkish. But they were all beautiful, and you could lift them out and put them back in different ways.

'It's lovely! I love it!'

'I knew you would! I told Mum you'd adore it.'

I kept on peeping at it all through the day, and took the time to pack it up again carefully before taking it home after the buzzer rang. I walked out of the gates to find Dad standing in the street, fiddling with his car keys. 'Oh, good! I was just wondering if I'd missed you. Hop in. Quick!'

'What's the hurry?'

'We're going shopping,' he told me. 'Laura is coming round for supper.'

'Really?'

'Yes, really. And we're going to cheat. We're going to that deli under the bridge.'

'The one Mum says is far, far too expensive?'

'Yes, that one. And your mother's right.'

Rainbow notebook

We argued all the way about what Laura might or might not want to eat. And then, when we arrived, Dad simply took the deli man's advice on everything – starters, main course and desserts.

On the way back to the car, I pulled Dad to a halt. 'Hang on!'

'What?'

I pressed my nose against the window of the gift shop we were passing, and pointed. 'That.'

'The stuffed bear?'

'No. That rainbow notebook.'

He squinted through the glass, and shrugged.

'Come on,' I said. 'We're going in.'

'Oh, Scarlet,' he wailed. 'We're in a hurry. Let's get back to the car.'

'No,' I insisted. 'I need that notebook.'

'Need it? How come? You get your school stuff from the office.'

'It's not for school.' I didn't want to explain, and anyway, I was already halfway through the door. 'Come on. You're going to have to lend me the money.'

'Scarlet . . .'

But he had lost the battle. Following me in, he dumped the shopping bags by the counter and waited while the owner reached into his display. He handed it to me. I flicked the pages to check they were blank. 'It's lovely. I'll take it.'

'Scarlet! You haven't even asked how much it costs.'

'It doesn't matter,' I told him. 'I'm going to pay you back.'

'That's not the point,' said Dad. 'It's not as if you even need it. That bright red notebook is already gathering dust on top of your wardrobe.'

I turned. 'How come you know that? Have you been *snooping*?'

Dad got on his high horse. 'I wouldn't dream of nosing into any of your private stuff. However, I do occasionally clean the house and that red book is hidden away up there where nobody would even think of looking. The vacuum nozzle knocked it off—'

'You haven't damaged it!'

'It's fine. It fell on the bed.' He lowered his voice so that the owner couldn't hear the next thing he said. 'Why don't you save your money? Leave this one here and—'

'No! I want this rainbow one.'

Dad gave up. Digging in his pocket, he produced his bank card. 'I warn you, I will make you pay me back.'

'That's fine. I will.'

On the drive home, he asked again, 'Why do you need two fancy blank notebooks anyway?'

I tapped the side of my nose. 'Secrets . . .'

He sighed. 'You are becoming a total woman of mystery.'

Interesting, that. Only a few weeks before, I know for sure he would have called me a child.

Easy together

It was an amazing supper. It wasn't even difficult to get it right. All the instructions for warming things through, and tipping the desserts out onto plates, were printed on the labels.

'And so they should be,' Dad said, 'at that price.'

Laura arrived just as we'd stuffed the packaging out of sight in the recycling. I think she was a bit surprised to see me, but she was friendly. She asked me whether Alice had got round to painting her room, and I said she was waiting till the end of term. We talked about Andy. She asked if his spinal problems were still on the mend, and I explained about Jake coming round and spinning that massive yarn to get Andy back to drama club before he even had time to think about it and get nervous.

She loved the idea of Jake having to think up, on the spot,

the name of a play with someone in a wheelchair. (I had to explain about the X-Men.) Then Dad told me and Laura a mangled version of some film that freaked him out when he was very young. I wasn't really listening. I think I was more watching the two of them, my dad and Laura, side by side on the sofa. She had her legs laid casually over his knees, and he was fiddling with her bracelets, spinning them gently round and round her wrist. I was reminded of the days when Alice and I both had long hair and I'd be stretched out on the sofa just the same way, with Alice fiddling with my hair, at times twisting the ends of it idly round and round her fingers, and sometimes braiding it properly.

They looked as comfortable as that. Easy together, like me and Alice have always been. And that's what gave me the confidence to ask, 'Laura, when am I ever going to meet your two giant sons?'

Dad snorted with amusement. 'Scarlet, they're not *that* big.'

Laura defended the way I'd put it. 'Compared to me, they are.' She gave my dad a wink before she turned back to me. 'And you'll be meeting them quite soon.'

She could have meant anything by that. Maybe just a restaurant meal. Maybe a party. Perhaps even a wedding. I wasn't horrified by any of the things that came to mind, so all I said was, 'Good.'

She smiled her very gentle smile. 'Because . . . ?'

'Alice,' I said. 'Alice is deadly curious, and keeps on nagging me to find out all about them.'

Dad shook his head. 'Your Alice!'

But Laura simply flattened her hand on my dad's thigh to lever herself more easily to her feet. 'I'm fetching the dessert.'

Scarlet stars and moons

After the rich peach meringues, I said that I had things to do and went upstairs to leave the two of them alone. We had no homework after the exams, so I just shoved a few revision papers away in files, then climbed on my chair to take the scarlet book down from the top of the wardrobe. I checked it carefully to see if Dad had spoiled the look of it, knocking it down. But it was fine. I used my pillowcase to give the cover a polish, and chose some wrapping paper from the rolls that Mum had left in Dad's hall cupboard.

I chose the pattern of scarlet stars and moons that matched it best, and wrapped the book with care. I put the package in a plastic bag to keep it clean and slid it in my school bag. And then at last I took my new, precious china nest of eggs out of its box to look at it again before I shouted down to Dad that I'd be having a shower, and going straight to bed.

He shouted up a cheerful goodnight. I think that Laura

did too. And I have no idea what time she left because, within an hour or so, I was asleep.

Nothing I'd miss

Dad dropped me back first thing in the morning.

'All sorted!' Mum told us proudly. 'The movers should be here in fifteen minutes.'

I looked around. The sink was shiny clean. A copy of the meter readings lay on the gleaming counter, and all the surfaces were clear. Every single thing we owned was packed into boxes, and the furniture was labelled: *Bedroom 1, Bedroom 2, Living room.*

'Your attic's cleaned out,' Mum told me. 'Nothing left to do there.'

But I still went upstairs, thinking it might be wise to check there were no lumps of gum stuck to the window frame. I peeled the fitted cushion off its Velcro backing and lifted it away from the tarnished brass hinge it hid so neatly. It was quite obvious that Mum had never found the secret place in which I'd kept the scarlet book. The hollow underneath the seat still held a handful of the stupid, funny notes that Alice and Jake had passed to me in class, and I had not chucked out.

I stuffed them deep in my pockets and looked around one last time. Would I regret the move? No, there was nothing I'd miss – not even the lovely curved perch in the window. In the new flat, I would be able to sit by the French doors. And in exciting weather, like the storms I'd watched from my porthole, I'd be able to push those doors open to feel the thrashing wind and smell the rain.

Another change. But I felt good about it – and maybe confident that there'd been enough change in me to fit in with the changes going on around me. I think I must have come down whistling because Mum said, sounding a little startled, 'Scarlet – you do sound happy.'

'I am,' I said. 'I love my little room in the new place. I love the steps down to my own private patch of garden. And I'll be nearer to Alice.'

Just then, the doorbell rang. The movers had arrived. Mum handed me some money and a set of keys I'd never seen before. 'If you go over there, and open up . . .'

'But won't you be ages?'

'They didn't think that it would take too long. But I'll be staying to do one last sweep through the house. So buy yourself a snack on the walk over, and make sure that you're there to let them in.' She handed me a sort of map. 'And try to keep the movers to the plan.'

I looked at what she'd given me. It clearly showed where all the heavier stuff should go in all the rooms. 'You're so efficient,' I teased her. 'You really ought to think of getting a job, like running a hospital.'

'Oh, Scarlet!' she laughed. But already one of the men was coming up to ask a question. 'I'll see you later,' she told me, turning to answer him.

Some sort of distance

I took my time, walking along behind the rows of back gardens. I wondered where in my room I'd ask the men to put my desk and bed. I thought about the sorts of posters I might put on my walls. I even wondered whether I could find another lamp like Andy's. I thought that would look good.

The locks turned easily. The flat was cool and clean. The first thing I did was fling the French doors open wide and gaze down at the garden. It somehow seemed even more bright and tangled than before. I wandered past the kitchen, and into my mind came the memory of hurling that mug of tea onto the floor because Dad had told me he was sure that things would not only turn out better for him and Mum but, in the end, for me.

Had he been right?

I wouldn't argue things were *better* now. But I didn't take it all the way I had before, as something unfair and selfish that had been done to me. I thought of it as something that had *happened*. I kept remembering what Jake had said when we were in that cupboard. 'Only small kids think everything's to do with them. Maybe you should *grow up*.'

I'd never tell him what he said had made a difference. But it had.

And I'd been having such a rush of happy confidence – even excitement – about this move to the flat. It wasn't anything to do with Mum breaking up with Richard, because I'd liked him, and if I'd had to have a sort of step-father, he would have been OK. No, I was ready to admit that things were all right because I'd come to see that I was old enough to keep some sort of distance from my parents' lives.

Which set me thinking . . .

Which set me thinking about Mum, and what spilled out of her that day she stood in the doorway to the living room and wouldn't even step inside to hand Richard his tea. That bitter remark she'd made about having to use up the bricks of your own life to build your children's lives instead.

I'd thought she was being so mean. Totally selfish. But

now I could see that all those sacrifices wouldn't be any sort of bargain unless the child you made them for finally turned into the sort of person you'd like to be around. I thought of Bev and Archie. I bet Bev glances into every mirror she passes and sees the bags under her eyes, and her greasy, unwashed hair, and still thinks that her precious Archie is worth it.

But if the child you're building up is always sour and self-obsessed you'd feel quite differently. I'd hate to think that I had sacrificed years of my life to put together a person I wouldn't even want to invite to tea.

It set me thinking about all the snide things I'd said to Mum after she'd told me she was leaving Dad. Sometimes I'd felt bad afterwards. Sometimes I hadn't. But getting at her had become almost a hobby. I'd barely missed a trick. And even when I had held off, I'd felt as if I had been doing her a favour she hadn't earned and didn't really deserve.

I tried to conjure up her face again, when she stood in that doorway. What was she thinking? Was she remembering back to when I was a chubby toddler like Archie, grabbing at everyone's hair and sleeves as I learned to walk? Was she comparing all the hopes she'd had back then with how I was turning out – so quick to mutter petty, spiteful things under my breath, so keen to catch her out in secrets and small deceptions. Hair-triggered to pick fights. Obviously she can't have been expecting something as easy-going (in its own way) as a plump baby who is being petted by three grown people grovelling on a carpet to amuse him.

But she had maybe hoped for more and better from me.

'What's up?'

After the men unloaded everything, and she had waved them off, Mum sent me out for more milk. When I came back, I found her perched on the edge of the sofa, staring into space.

'What's up?' I asked her. 'Have they broken something important?'

She shook her head. 'No, no. They did a fine job.'

'You look washed out, though. Shall I make some tea?'

'I haven't started to unpack the kitchen stuff.'

That did surprise me. Last time we'd moved, she'd had the kitchen shipshape in no time at all.

'Is anything wrong?' A nasty thought struck. 'You're not regretting coming here?'

'Oh, no. Not that.' Still, she did sigh. 'I think I've just been feeling a bit besieged.'

'Besieged?'

'I can't explain.' She tossed her head like someone in a swimming pool shaking water from their ears. 'I feel a bit beaten up – as if I'm at the end of a very long journey. I've just been sitting here trying to get it together to start on the unpacking. But . . .'

Her eyes filled up. The tears rolled down her cheeks.

'Stay there!' I said. 'Don't move. I'll find the tea stuff.'

It wasn't difficult. She'd obviously still had her usual grip on things while she'd been packing at the other end. In the kitchen a few small cardboard boxes had been left on top of bigger cartons, and inside the third one I found the kettle, a box of tea bags and some mugs.

Out

After her second cup, Mum claimed she felt much better. 'I'm fine now. Really. I'll get on with things.'

I took control. 'No, not tonight. We'll just sort out the bedding, then we'll go out for supper. We can unpack tomorrow.'

'But I'll be at work.'

'That doesn't matter. We can do a bit when we get home, and sort the rest out later, when we have the time.'

'No, really, Scarlet. I think we ought—'

'No,' I said firmly. 'We are going *out*.'

And that was what we did.

A present for you

I waited till the waiter had taken our order, then slid the package across the table. 'Here. It's a present for you.'

She looked down at the shiny moons and stars. 'A present?'

'A sort of house-warming present,' I explained. 'I think you need it more than I do now.'

'What is it?' She was peeling off the sticky tape the way she always does, trying to save the wrapping paper so she can recycle it.

'Go mad,' I ordered her. 'Just tear off the paper and look.'

The paper fell away, revealing the scarlet book, as bright and shiny and as beautiful as it had been the day she gave it to me.

Mum looked up, startled. 'So can I read it now?'

'Yes,' I said. 'You can read everything inside it.'

The blood drained from her face, as if she'd only just that second realized that seeing what I might have written in the scarlet book about my feelings in the last few weeks would be the very last straw on such a tiring day. If I was being nasty, then she couldn't bear it.

But Mum's no quitter. She took a breath and flipped it open. Two blank pages opposite one other. She turned another page. The same. She started flicking pages back and forth. Blank, blank, blank, blank. 'But this is totally *unused*,' she said. 'There's nothing in it.'

'No,' I said. 'That's why I'm giving it to you.'

'I don't understand.'

'Neither did I,' I told her. 'When you first gave it me, I thought you wanted me to use it so you could find out what I was thinking – use it to spy on me. It's only later that I thought maybe that wasn't what you had in mind at all. Maybe you simply wanted me to have somewhere to put down all my worries and irritations and hopes for the future. Maybe you thought that would help.'

Mum was just looking at me, not saying a word.

I carried on. 'And perhaps it would have helped, except that I refused to do it. I hid the book away. And all this time has passed. But I don't need it any more. I'm fine. Everything's going well at school, and with Dad, and with you, and with Alice.' (I nearly added, 'And with Jake', but dropped that at the last moment.) 'So I am giving it back to you.'

Mum gave me a rather watery smile. 'Why? So that I can write down all my worries and irritations?'

'And hopes for the future,' I suggested. 'Anything. Knowing the way your mind works, you could use it to make a list of things you're going to do.'

'Do?'

'Yes. Now that you're on your own. Like learn Italian, or take singing lessons. Join a tennis club. Get a puppy. Take me on holiday to Greece. Anything.'

She gave me another of those rueful smiles. 'You make it all sound really good and optimistic.'

'It is,' I said. 'Why shouldn't it be? Wasn't it you who told me that a woman needs a man like a fish needs a bicycle?'

'Yes, I suppose I did.'

'And aren't you the one who's always quoting the statistic that single women are healthier and happier than married women?'

'Yes,' she admitted. 'I guess that's me as well.'

'So make the most of being single,' I said. 'After all, it might not last. And in the evenings, when you're not out with a walking group, or brushing up your French, or playing badminton, or whatever, you can write in the scarlet book.'

'I can,' she said. 'In fact, I think I will.'

I watched Mum wrap the scarlet book up safely in the crumpled paper and slide it in her bag. She reached across the table to pat my hand. 'Thanks, Scarlet.' Her eyes were brimming again, but luckily at that moment our poppadoms arrived, along with all those little pots of dips.

'Yum,' I said. 'I *adore* poppadoms. We ought to eat out far more often, Mum. I'm always saying that.'

'So you are,' Mum said, and she smiled at me through what was left of her tears.

Here am I

So far as I know, Mum's never written in the scarlet book. She hasn't had the time. But here am I, sprawled on my stomach in my own tiny garden and writing in my battered rainbow one. I've almost filled it up, trying to tell this story as honestly as I can. And simply setting it down I can quite easily see how difficult I must have been to live with at times, especially at the start. But I can truly say that the upheaval came as a massive surprise. I know when anyone looks round, they see separation and divorce because it's everywhere. I told you, half my own class come from split homes – some twice over.

Still, I don't think I ever really expected that it would happen to me. Like the Henty family's car crash (even if nowhere near as bad) it came as an awful shock.

But we are all OK now. All of us. I look at Mum, and it does seem to me that she's much better off than she was at the start, even with far less money. She gets her hair done more often. She wears her nicest clothes, even to work. Instead of keeping her phone tucked underneath her chin and making endless calls to people at work, she listens to the radio while tidying round, or keeping Sajid's mum's garden just as nice as it was when we first moved in. (Nicer, in places.) She's joined a book group, and there's another gang of women she meets quite often. She hasn't managed to explain exactly what they do, so I suspect that they just gather in bars and talk about their jobs and have a laugh about their husbands and ex-mates.

She's happy now. I hear her singing as she cooks. I know she's feeling far more confident, and even though she says she's no idea what's going to happen in the future, that doesn't seem to bother her at all. Jake has let drop that his uncle's moved into the place he lent to us, and has a house-mate now. 'But he is just some guy from work.' All Mum said was, 'I'm so glad that's worked out. Because I did feel bad, giving him so little warning that we were leaving.'

She's never mentioned it again, so I'm as sure as I can be that she's not pining. And when Richard Naylor drove past Alice and me and Andy in the street a few days ago, and honked at us and waved, he didn't look unhappy either. Andy called back at us, 'Whoa, guys!' (We were racing his wheelchair so as not to miss the start of the film.) 'Who on earth was that?'

'That was Jake's famous uncle,' Alice said, and added brutally, 'Just water under the bridge.'

'Bit harsh,' I said. But I suppose, as usual, Alice is right,

Things past, things present, things to come

As for my dad, he seems content enough. He hasn't tried to start things up again with Mum. I'm not at all convinced that what he has going with Laura is what you'd call a 'passion'. Sometimes I think the main thing he likes about her is that she's so nice and easy, and keeps him from feeling that he's on his own. Even when Laura's not around, the house feels brighter and more cheerful. I've got a lot more of my stuff at Mum's, but I'm still cosy at Dad's.

I've no idea if he will stay in our old house. I overheard him and Laura talking about possibly switching the second name on the mortgage to hers when Dad gives Mum her final share next month. But maybe he'll simply decide to move somewhere smaller instead. I don't think that I care.

I wouldn't want to leave this lovely flat, though. I asked Mum if we'd have to move again, and she said no. 'We'll keep on renting till Sajid's ready to sell, and then we'll pounce.' She says we'll stay in it at least till I'm finished with my education – hopefully longer.

Alice is thrilled. She acts as if without her nagging me, Mum and I would have made a terrible mistake and spent the rest of our lives shivering in some dank and overpriced hole, sobbing in our soup. It's the first place that she dragged Andy to when being back at drama club cheered him enough to start going other places. I heard her bullying him. 'There will be no excuses! Either we take the portable ramp, or you can stagger up three steps on crutches. Just decide.'

He chose the crutches. I kicked the rugs out of his way, and when he smiled at me in thanks, I suddenly remembered why I had always got along with him so well before the accident. Mum left a heap of sandwiches and made some feeble excuse to leave. And then, to my astonishment, Jake showed up. (Alice: 'Oh! So sorry, Scarlet! Did I forget to tell you I'd invited him as well? You don't mind, do you?')

She didn't even try to make it sound like a real question. And, no, I didn't mind. They're all three of them round here often now. We sit in a row on the steps, looking down to my little private garden, trying to stop Archie pulling off all the bright blossoms. We talk about all sorts of things – things past, things present, things to come.

And I am happy. Yes, it all worked out. And I am happy too.

About the Author

Anne Fine is a distinguished writer for both adults and children. She has twice been voted Children's Author of the Year, and became Children's Laureate in 2001. In 2003 she was made a Fellow of the Royal Society of Literature and was awarded an OBE. Her work has been translated into over forty languages.

Anne is one of five daughters, and has written a good deal about the stresses – and amusements – of family life. The comedy film *Mrs Doubtfire* is based on her novel *Madame Doubtfire*, and amongst other adaptations of her work, the BBC filmed her Smarties Prize-winning *Bill's New Frock*. As well as many other regional and foreign prizes, Anne won the Guardian Children's Fiction Prize for *Goggle-Eyes*, along with Britain's most coveted award for children's literature, the Carnegie Medal. She won the Carnegie Medal again for *Flour Babies*, which also won the Whitbread/Costa Children's Book of the Year Award, and the publication of *The Tulip Touch* brought her a second Whitbread/Costa Award.

Another Whitbread/Costa winner published by DFB is Linda Newbery, who won the award for her novel, *Set in Stone*. Another of Linda's books, *The Key to Flambards*, is the sequel to K.M. Peyton's much acclaimed *Flambards* series (the second novel of which, *The Edge of the Cloud*, also won the Carnegie Medal).

A *Books for Keeps* Book of the Year

Linda Newbery brings K.M. Peyton's legendary *Flambards* series into the present day.

Fourteen-year-old Grace, recovering from a life-changing accident and her parents' divorce, reluctantly spends the summer at Flambards, a remote country house. Despite herself, she befriends two local boys: Jamie, who is friendly and obsessed with wildlife, and Marcus, who is struggling to deal with his moody, potentially violent father.

In this beautiful but threatened landscape, Grace unearths her own extraordinary ties to the house and – importantly – discovers her own place in the world.

So much had changed in the last year and a half that Grace felt her old life had been torn into bits and fed through a shredder. First, Mum and Dad's split, after several months of will-they-won't-they, with Grace caught in the middle, not wanting to take sides but trying to take both sides at once. That had been bad enough.

And then that day – that May evening that severed Grace's life into Before and After. That day that should have been marked on the calendar with a big red WARNING sign and flashing lights.

The day of It.

Since then, she'd gone over and over the small things and ordinary decisions that had funnelled her into It, as if It was meant to happen. Without any one of them, the day would have been as unremarkable as any other Thursday, not particularly remembered. If only it had been raining, then she wouldn't have gone out for a run. If only she'd decided to go the other way to the park, through the alleyways, as she often did. If only her maths homework had been harder, taking her a few minutes longer to work through – a few minutes, *a few minutes* would have made all the difference between what happened and what so easily needn't have.

If only the Peugeot driver had taken another route. If only he'd stopped to fill up with petrol or buy chocolate. If only the traffic lights had changed to red a moment sooner. If only he'd been concentrating, not laughing with the woman in the passenger seat, singing along to loud music as he came round the corner too fast, much too fast, beating the red light.

Any of those things could have been different, but they weren't, and never would be. No matter how many times she replayed, it was always the same – herself running along the pavement, the red Peugeot turning right at the junction, the two of them pulled together as if by a powerful magnet.

The moment when the engine sound became more than that of passing traffic. The car swerving straight at her. The driver's hands wrenching the wheel, the woman passenger open-mouthed in horror.

I'm dead, Grace thought, trapped by a high wall to her right. She could still recall the instant in which she was able to think that quite calmly.

But next moment she twisted away and leaped, for a wild second thinking she'd jumped clear—

Then the impact, the sickening slam. The car bucked forward as it struck. Her head and shoulder crunched hard against the bonnet. Searing pain carried her away on a dark wave.

That was all she could remember. Letting the merciful darkness wash over her, drown her. Dying must be like that.

Afterwards, everyone said she was lucky not to have been killed. If she hadn't been pinned against the wall, she could have been flung right through the windscreen.

Lucky.

That depended how you looked at it, and she certainly didn't feel lucky.

Somehow she was still alive, but they couldn't save her leg.

She was too drugged and groggy after the emergency operation to take it in properly. It was Mum who told her in words that seemed meaningless, nothing to do with her as she floated in and out of sleep. 'You're here, that's the most important thing,' Mum kept saying, with a sob in her voice. 'And we love you, we'll always be here. We'll get through this.'

Dad was there too, she was sure he was. Did that mean they were together again?

Much later – hours or days, she couldn't tell – she was suddenly awake, staring at the ceiling. She registered that she was still in hospital. Did she live here now? Dad was slumped by her bed in a chair, making a small whistling sound as he snored. A drip thing was attached to her arm;

she felt a dull pain in her hand, and saw the bandage that held the tube in place and the bag of liquid suspended on a metal stand.

They'd said something about losing her leg, or had she only dreamed that? It was the sort of thing that happened in a nightmare and then you'd wake up, flooded with relief because you were in your own bed and everything was the same as usual. When she glanced down she saw the shape of her left leg – thigh, knee, waggle-able foot – all perfectly normal under the thin blanket; then a cagey shape over the other. So it was there, then. But she kept puzzling, knowing they wouldn't say that unless it were true. How could her leg be gone?

No. No. They couldn't chop off part of her. She needed two legs; everyone did. How would she walk? Run? How would she be herself? She tried to wiggle her toes, but only felt heaviness there. Her mind blurred in panic and disbelief.

'Dad. Dad! Wake up!'

'Hmmnn?' He pushed himself up, blinking.

'My – my leg. What's happened?'

'Oh, Gracey.' He leaned close, cuddling her. 'Sweetheart.' He could only force the words out with difficulty. 'They – they couldn't save it. It was too badly crushed. They had to amputate below the knee. You've still got your knee.'

Even though it didn't seem real, she found herself sobbing, holding him tight, smelling the clean cotton of his shirt and a faint sweatiness and soap while he rocked her.

She knew he was crying too, and trying not to. At least he didn't tell her she was lucky.

My leg, she thought, *my leg!* It seemed the most precious part of her. It'd be sports day soon – she'd need her leg back by then. How would she run the 200 metres, the 4x100 metres relay? How could they take part of her body away? What had they done with it?

One moment the truth of her situation thudded into her; next instant it skittered away, impossible to grasp.

Days followed days of hospital, rehabilitation, physiotherapy. Marie-Louise came to visit, often; so, once, did some of her other friends from school, Carrie and Jenna and Luke. She didn't know what she wanted from them. Not sympathy: 'Oh, how awful,' Carrie kept saying, her eyes filling with tears. 'I can't imagine what it must be like.' (I know, Grace wanted to say, but perhaps you could *try?*) Jenna talked only about herself, as if the whole subject of Grace's accident were best avoided; and Luke kept saying how cool it was, how Grace could be a blade runner and win medals in the Paralympics. 'Tokyo, twenty-twenty. You'll have three years to train.' And, 'What happened to your leg, after they cut it off? Did it have its own funeral?' which struck Grace as just *sick*.

Marie-Louise was the only one she really wanted to see. Marie-Louise, who wanted to be a doctor, seemed to understand that Grace didn't want tears, or sorrow, or constant questions, and they had the kind of special friendship that meant they didn't need to talk all the time. She brought books and magazines, and chocolate truffles her mother had made. She talked about prosthetic limbs and how people got used to them, as if all this were quite normal. As if there were a huge but perfectly manageable job to do, and she'd be there to help, all the way.

There were times when Grace hated her body, wished she could slip out of it. It was spoiled for ever, broken, incomplete. Instead of a right shin and foot, her leg – swollen, multi-coloured with bruising – ended in a smooth stump below the knee. She could hardly bear to look, though the stump received constant attention to check that it was healing well, and had its own special shrinker sock to bring down the swelling.

Stored on her phone was a photo she couldn't help looking at, though it felt like being kicked in the stomach. It had been taken by Marie-Louise at the start of term, on the running track in the school field. There stood Grace – the old Grace, as she couldn't help thinking of herself now – lined up with three others, eager, smiling into the sun. She wore a vest and Lycra shorts; her legs were long and slim.

Legs. Both of them. Two; a pair. Ready to run. How fantastic it had been to have two fully functioning legs. She thought now that she should have been grateful for that, every single one of those days when she'd never given it a thought.

When she remembered running, lived it, *felt* it with all her senses – she wanted to wail and howl. How could that have been taken away from her? The very worst thing she could have lost. Running was more than just running. It was who she was.

This is me. Running.

Now? *That* was *me. That was the real me, not this wreck of a person. How can I get the old me back?*

Looking at the photograph through a mist of tears, she poised her thumb to delete it, but couldn't. To do that would be to lose herself, her self. Fit, athletic Grace. Where was she now?

I can't let go of her. Can't give in. That would make it real.

'It's all right, it's all right to cry,' said Nurse Liz, Grace's favourite, with her corkscrew curls that sprang out from a tight ponytail and her big smile that could quickly turn to seriousness. When Grace sobbed, 'It's not fair, it's not fair!' Nurse Liz agreed that no, it wasn't fair at all.

There were greater unfairnesses in the world, Grace knew; no one had any special right to go through life untroubled, undamaged. But that knowledge couldn't cut through her grief.

'You were just unlucky. In the wrong place at the wrong time.' She lost count of the number of people who told her that. It was the *just* that got her, that sneaky little word that crept in everywhere. Too bad, it meant. Put up with it. There's no choice.